TH VOYAGES OF CAPTAIN NED

ODES TO A SAILOR

D H Wells

This edition published in Great Britain in 2014 by

MyVoice Publishing
Matlock Court
34 Meads Street
EASTBOURNE
BN20 7QY

ISBN 978-1-909359-43-7

Driftwood Books

Introduction

David Wells was a sailor. You can tell that as soon as you begin to read the book. His twenty year career in the Merchant Navy spanned the globe and his deep love of the sea and the infinite depths of his nautical lore ebb through every page. He may not have sailed before the mast, but his first mentors did.

This authenticity creates a spell-binding read, of the sort you can only get from somebody who knows his subject with a combination of fact and fantasy. David Wells describes the Days of Sail with a painstaking, loving hand that breathes life into the pages. You leave the book feeling enriched with the knowledge of what it was truly like to sail the Seven Seas in the heyday of the British Empire, not as a Royal Navy Jack Tar, but as an ordinary sailor on a working ship.

The book is written as an ode, an unfashionable style, but memorable and perfectly suited for this story. It sweeps you along and before long you don't notice the poetry as you are enveloped in the story.

Walking the decks of the sailing ship 'Cutty Sark' or similarly preserved vessels, it is easy to imagine the exciting and frightening life of the men who sailed these ships.

Captain Ned is a fictitious sailing ship master and his experiences are sometimes outrageous... the excitement and danger is ever present as David Wells brings to life the past with unerring skill.

Rex Sumner
Critic, Author and Publisher

Contents

First Command

He sailed out of port most skilfully, now getting familiar with this piece of sea.
With all sails independently set, to catch the wind from tack to tack.

The channel mark he should have closed a little sooner – but not too easy on a three masted schooner: he didn't want her to run too far as he turned the head of the *"DARTFORD STAR"*
For on the port bow a long mud spit – with a marker called The Bamboo Stick.
The water now deep but still many shallows, the worst bit known as The Cartwheel Narrows.

Finally set on a course for the great beyond, known by mariners as The Big Deep Pond. The captain sighed with great satisfaction, a clean run through thanks to timely action.

****

A packet called the *"MALLARD"*, fine on the starboard bow hauled away sharply from the *"STAR'S"* sharp prow; and three small craft followed where the mother-ship led, and gave a wide berth to Captain Ned.

On the horizon, a full set of sails moving towards us tho' a head wind prevails. A ship-of-the-line, still in her prime easily identified as a ship of the White

Swan Line. Of massive proportion… approach with caution and in a seaman-like way – give her more sea room.

We've had a good run on the open sea; clips along when running free. But now she's approaching a dangerous place – a current on Ned's chart called The Old Mill Race.

"Helm hard up to the starboard tack"

Then suddenly he's coming under attack. Missiles rain down out of the sky… one near miss.

"A **pathetic** try"

No real cause for any alarm – nothing to really cause much harm.
It's coming from the wooded shore, and he's had some trouble around here before… from a band of pirates known as The Brothers Jim… Ned will be having a few words with them.

But now a problem, dreaded at sea – the shore **dangerously** close on the port side lee… and just in time a voice called out.

"**Time for tea**!" …and bring young Jimmy with you"

He tucked the "*STAR*" up under his arm …Another voyage on his grandfather's farm.

Promotion

We next meet our man on a Chinese sampan.
Strange you might ask, a simple task for a man
trained to sail the deep ocean.
But that was the state of the brave second mate
who'd experienced degrading demotion.

In a rotten old barque from Bristol they'd sailed and
trouble was there from the start –

Led by a mate-hating Scouse the crew gave Ned a
hard time. Leaving halyards slack and slow changing
tack; late on watch, the lanterns unlit.

To show who was boss Ned made an example... and
hung the Scouse by his boots from the bowsprit.

The Captain took a dim view, reduced Ned to the
crew complete with his books and his bedding.

So once in Foo Chow he'd try every how to get work
away from that barque. And our very proud man
served as mate on a sampan – a rotten old heap and
the pay very cheap but it covered his food and his
lodging.

Down on his luck and feeling the rub he looked for
solace in a riverside pub.
When up on his knee slid young Rosie Lee.

"I'm all yours for the night for a shilling"

Ned sighed, and gazed into her innocent young eyes
and saw sweetness and kindness and love.

"Don't be offended my dear, I'm only here for the
beer and in this kind of mood… I'm really not willing"

She beamed a big smile in her Oriental style and
said that she "Quite understood"

"If it's a ship you are needing – I've heard on the vine
that a clipper ship's sailing and must be on time…
and the mate is late or gone missing"

Ned hurried along to the quay full of clippers –
famous names and infamous skippers.
And then he found her, a fine 'homeward bounder'
loading tea in every great hold.

Up on the gangway in uniform dressed the 2nd mate
greeted in a way that impressed.

"So pleased if you join us, we're missing some crew
and to sail so short-handed just wouldn't do.
Welcome to the "Flying Goose"
You'll meet the old captain , don't be put off by his
manner: a **hard**-driving man. A tight fisted Scotsman
who's frequently drunk… he'll break every rule…
stand as firm as you can"

Captain Mactweedie, as wide as he's tall, with a
snowy white beard hanging half to the floor, all

stained at the edges from smoking a pipe – squinty black eyes beneath a cap far too tight.

"I'll give you the job laddie as my new First Mate – but half the pay will have to dooo… We're a homeward bounder, and you need me – much more than I need yooo"

"The man you're replacing was weak and feeble and well over the hill. And has apparently succumbed to the charms of old Shanghai Lil."

"They've rolled him and robbed him – they took his fine boots, his trousers, his watch and Havana cheroots.
So I hope ye're God fearing, tough and quite willing, for I'll push this old girl to earn every last shilling.
Passengers we've but twooo. It'll just have to dooo and it all helps to make a small profit"

             ****

"Let's stroll the decks and I'll make my checks"
Said Ned to the 2nd. Mate Peter.

"She's a good looking ship and with her fine raking bow, I doubt that many could beat her'

"That may be true" Peter replied, looking around a little bit nervous.

"But Mactweedie is greedy, he cuts things too tight. Half the crew have gone missing… they disappeared

in the night.
He's filled the apprentice boy's cabin with boxes of
tea – no way to treat youngsters just starting at sea.
He sold the pig to the mate of a brig and the chickens
unfed are looking quite sickly.
The potatoes are rot and the man should be shot for
sailing without fresh drinking water".

****

"Captain Mactweedie – a word if I may. We're sailing
short-handed and I don't think we ought-to leave
without fresh food and good drinking water."

Mactweedie he fumed and stomped around the
saloon, banging the table and spilling his over-large
tot.
His face went quite purple – Ned thought he might
die... a chance for promotion, really quite high.

"Just listen now mister, I don't care what ye think,
ignore all the rumours, they're false and they stink.
No time for storing, we sail on the tide, if water we
are missing – the good Lord will provide.
We'll push her hard mister, I know all the ways. I
want to reach London in one hundred and five days".

Ned understood the reason, he'd been reliably told –
the first tea ashore is worth more than gold.

"Meet the passengers now, and be most polite, no
sound of your whinging, or you'll find ah can fight".

First Lady Ford-Chumley, who was really quite comely, her hair combed high on her head. But at six foot two without stockings or shoes, she could hardly fit into her bed.

Then a parson in dog-collar, cassock and hat, carrying an ivory bound prayer book and with a complexion to match.

****

They sailed in the night – Mactweedie wouldn't be late, and steered sou,sou,west for Borneo and the old Sunda Strait.
They took a short cut on the Middleton Bank, surrounded by reefs on which others had sunk.

"D'ye know this way mister?" Mactweedie asked. "It requires nerve and skill – but it gains us some miles. It's a course ye must hold… if I'm ta win ma bonus of gold".

Four in the morning and Ned's feeling just right; stars fill the heavens – a magnificent sight.
Creaming along, bounding along, a list to the lee; an incredible eighteen knots, with a following sea.
Stud sails and sky sails to catch every breeze… Mactweedie's gold?... We should win it with ease.

But trouble was brewing; it grew stiflingly hot.
The crew are complaining of thirst and of grub.

The Chinese cook, Charlie Chang, making chicken

feet stew, was ordered to use salt water and the stew turned to glue.

In the saloon that night things came to a head, the issue being the lack of fresh water.
The captain said grace adding:-

"Lord, provide for my crew: put an end to these rumours, there is no concealment, they've got all they need".

Too much for Ned!

"Not the good Lord Sir, **YOU** Sir should provide food and water – when they signed on you agreed; there'll be a price you will pay for your cheating and greed".

With the taste of the soup her Ladyship puked and the parson choked on a potato.
Mactweedie stormed off, his face looking evil... he'll seek his revenge... all things being equal.

On watch that night Ned was having a pee in the starboard side scupper, when her Ladyship stepped up on the poop. She smoked a cheroot and was drinking pink gin and worried our Ned with a salacious, broad grin.

"Hello dear Ned – are you of good cheer?
I'm sorry I disturbed you... but I didn't see you were having a pee... let's pretend I never observed you.
It's terribly hot and I just couldn't sleep – this skirt is so heavy... I've nothing beneath!"

Her eyes they narrowed and she puckered her lips
and her fingers fumbled with the belt on her hips.

Ned leapt to the rail, his head in a tizzy.

"Excuse me my Lady, I'm really quite busy"

"Oh Ned stop pretending, the ship sails with ease;
you're a red-blooded male... I'm a woman... with
needs"

****

Deep in the Indian Ocean, unbearably hot – the seas
turning rough and causing commotion. Pots and
pans they went flying – the chickens are dying and
the cat – fell from the cross-trees.

Mactweedie was happy – she was bounding along,
making twenty one knots in the stiffening breeze.
But the crew grew resentful: It would be nice to be
first, but not if you're smelly and dying of thirst.

That night things would happen that would change
young Ned's life.
It began in the saloon, Mactweedie sharpening a
knife... to carve the last chicken (found dead in the
hutch)
So skinny and dry, they wouldn't get much.

"Sir – I respect your hard-driving but I must say
again, the crew are stinking and thirsty... we must
look for rain"

Lady Ford-Chumley cut in as the tensions heightened.
"I must confess – the smell of men's sweat makes me feel quite excited"

Then on watch things began to happen. The wind grew squally, clouds started to thicken and on the port horizon... RAIN... It made Ned's heart quicken.

"Helm down a bit – haul on those braces; you've got to be quick with fickle rain chases"

They steered for a hole in a tunnel of cloud – the sky growing blacker; the squall testing the mainsails and shrouds.
The heavens then opened:
The rain poured down the face of the sails and repeatedly filled the line-up of pails.
Soon the casks were full enough but the crew wanted some fun, they'd drunk until bursting, their washing was done.
And with just trilby hats on and as silly as kids, they ran around in the buff.

Lady Ford-Chumley appeared on the deck: She was completely **nude!** Save for some beads round her neck.

"I'm sorry Ned, but it's too hot in bed, please do not think that I'm rude!"

She joined the sailors dancing; they were shocked and confused, with her large breasts a-swinging...

the apprentice boys thrilling, **they** were amused.

"Hello boys, put away your toys, I'm a real woman through and through. Let's play a game... how about chase and catch, once around the capstan and the small booby hatch... (giggle)... Winner takes all"

Then at the moment of Ned's utter surprise (he thought he was dreaming) Mactweedie chose to arrive.
He had a knot in his beard and was clearly quite drunk. Wearing only his cap and grubby long-John's, he'd been thrown clean out of his bunk.

"Are you **crazy** or just useless?"

He roared at a wide-eyed Ned.

"You've lost more than ten miles... You'll **wish** you were dead"

And at the moment Mactweedie raised his big fist – the parson crowned him with a metal fish dish.

Back on course and creaming along; her stern dipping down to a southerly swell, Ned fixed a position – half way, as best he could tell.

****

Then from somewhere behind him a sight to be seen, Mactweedie arrived – pointing a finger with a blood-curdling scream... unlike his usual, insulting bark; for

coming up from windward, the unmistakable shape –
the grand *"CUTTY SARK"*.

By next noon she had passed them – Captain
Mactweedie was having a fit.

"They're after ma gold – it makes me feel sick. Press
on Mister Neddy – use every sail, this situation **must
not** prevail. Use the Parson's cassock, use the
bosun's sheets. If we do not catch her… the thought
makes me greet."

By morning the tea clipper was clean out of sight,
and the top sails are shredding to add to their plight.
When a mountainous sea she was about to ride:
Mactweedie appeared and jumped clean over the
side.
In that situation now't can be done – all sailormen
accept it, under the sun.

****

Now Ned is the captain: It's more than he'd dare
hope.

"So square up my lads, for the Cape of Good Hope."

They made a good passage, found the south-
easterly Trades, avoided the doldrums but the speed
they could not raise.

The tea price will be handsome it's the height of new

fashion, but unlike the first ship they'll not have to ration.

****

They raced up the Atlantic, they pushed hard and were bold but not quite sufficient to win Ned the gold.

The ship is going to owners anew; and jobs for young captains are **very** few.

So it was time to say his good-byes… and our young Ned was in for another surprise.
As he knocked, her door opened.

"I just wanted to say…"

But the words choked him. Lady Ford-Chumley and the parson were in-flagrante.

****

A Crew For The 'Cross-Eyed Raven'

Captain Ned stared at the deck above his bunk and guessed life would be tough; the splits and leaks in the tired old teak was looking rather rough.

"'Tis a crew I need" He sighed as he slipped into his blue serge trousers.
"But who would sail on this old girl, other than crooks and rebel-rousers?"

With his salt stained cap and rolled up map he headed for the gangway – and at the end of the quay he could clearly see a pub with likely credentials. The Olde Ship Inn with its smell and its din, drunken sailors and tarts – a bald parrot that farts and other seafaring essentials.

"Tell me," He said to the barmaid called Fred; Fredrika to those who she fancied.

"I'm in need of a crew, any will do, if they've two legs and can handle a mainsail. I've a cargo you see that's waiting for me and the shipper's becoming impatient"

Fred leaned on the bar and with a sweep of her hand spread ale all over the floor. The old timber groaned at her twenty-two stone and the parrot it shifted its perch. Her lipstick bright red, to her teeth it had

spread, all gold and the centre one missing; blonde hair and large earrings, a dress pitch black, deep cut and revealing and an eye-patch to match... and hands like a bunch of bananas.
She lit a cheroot.

"What's in it for me?"

She asked with a voice that was deep.

"After all" and she smiled, "I've a reputation to keep."

"A tenner my dear and never you fear, your reputation is safe in my hands. Just a few lads, no force or Shanghai... maybe a **little** persuasion."

She rang the bell, so the men could tell this would be a special occasion. The noise it subdued and they peered through the gloom, for they knew better than test her; her feats in the ring – a jaw-breaking punch and champion arm wrestler.

"Pay attention boys... Your slates are run out; with the rum and the gin and the gallons of stout. You've enjoyed all my kindness, the girls and the grub; you'll never find better than my homely old pub. So pay up and be grateful, you've enjoyed your last kip – I've got you some earnings... a fine sailing ship."

The bosun he opened a watery old eye and searched for his wallet beneath a prostitute's thigh.

"What be she?" He challenged our Fred; for an old

salt like he knew good ships from bad and the easier sailing was the one to be had.

"The *CROSS-EYED RAVEN.*"

With a crash and a roar, they raced for the door… 'twas the name that every Jack dreaded. But Fred was ahead with her arms and legs spread.

"Get back!" She yelled and it filled them with fear. "First you must pay for your lodgings and beer."

And her fee went up by a fiver.

She raised the bar slate for all to see and the cabin boy made an involuntary pee – for just like the others he was hugely in debt and now all he had was months to regret.

Ned paid off their slate and led them on board and Fred watched at the gangway in case one should run, a cosh in her hand – she was having such fun.

They sailed on the tide – a sorrowful sight, her dirty old sails all patched and worn, no use at the Cape or in the mildest of storm.

Ned mustered the crew and read them the rules.

"I know that the Raven's not the one you would choose; but that is life, some you win some you lose… So set-to and be grateful and don't you forget, I'm the one who settled your debt."

With a chuckle he descended to his cabin below…
just as the old girl made her first westerly lurch… the
bald headed parrot fell off its temporary perch.

"What you doing here? (Ned asked) I think you've
made a mistake"

"No he hasn't." (Said a voice from his shadowy bunk)

He turned and was startled at the sight of that hunk.

"Come over and join me (and she patted her thigh)
It's your lucky day captain… you've won the first
prize.

****

Via The Cape To Valparaiso

They headed south to catch the Trades, a wind that's pretty reliable. Then west a bit for South America's tip...and the dreaded Roaring Forties.

Captain Ned was pleased with his motley new crew and they needed little coercion, on account of the presence of a woman on board... the one-eyed fearful new bosun.

"Get aloft!" yelled Fred with a sadistic smile that curled her full red lips.
"The last one to pass gets a kick up the arse and the smallest portion for dinner."

"Dinner?" said Bill, as he edged out on the yard to lower yet more sails.
"Salt pork and hard duff, it's hardly enough, for a man needs his strength to handle this wench, in those endless southerly gales."

"You're doing just fine," said Ned to the bar-maid from Devon.
"And I see that the parrot has got a new feather. But a little kindness my dear would give much cheer to the boys before we meet bad weather."

Fred let out a sigh and gazed with one eye at the man who had won her affection. She adjusted his tie and patted his cap, almost knocking him senseless –

she had the strength of five horses.

"Just leave 'em to me, I know what is best. Look after the compass, the charts and the courses. They'll get no peas, no sausage or gravy – give 'em too much and you'll just make them lazy."

The temperature dropped and the sky clouded over; a southerly swell hinted at what would be waiting… as they closed on the Cape… there'd be no abating.

The fo'c'sle became forlorn – cold and damp and had a very bad smell. Too many men cramped in that airless peak… a veritable version of hell.

The cabin boy curled up in his bunk, with snoring and farting from the bunks up above. He dreamed of old Devon, green hills and lost love.

"All hands aloft!" screamed Fred from the hatch. In shining black oilskins and a sou'wester to match. "Bring in the mainsail and set a new jib… Move at the double, like you've just moments to live!"

"Jump to it!" squawked the parrot, its new feather wrapped around its tummy to keep out the cold. "A storm, it is coming – or so I am told."

The crew they cursed as they hauled in the sails – or all that was left of that rotten old cloth, patched and re-patched and chewed by the moth.
The price they were paying for cheap booze and soft women… the vicar had warned them, the price of

their sinning.

"Get more sail!" bawled Fred who was getting quite anxious.
"The barometer's dropping and tells of a storm – 'tis what one expects when rounding the Horn."

Wide-eyed and real frightened, the sailmaker's face, when he confronted the bosun, he showed her no grace.

"No good you shouting for more and for more – the last piece just left my mouldy old store."

"We've a problem my dear," said Fred to the captain. "The sails that are set will not last the night. If we don't hold our course we'll be in terrible plight.

Ned scratched his rain soaked head and looked for an answer… in the wardrobes and lockers, beneath his cosy old bed, and then… 'inspiration'!

"We'll need a needle and thread."

The crew they were huddled in the lee of the galley and watched the seas surging from mountain to valley.

"We're doomed!" wailed the cook. And the old ship lay on her creaking beam ends.
"Old Neptune he wants us – it's the message he sends."

When out on the deck stepped the captain and Fred
with an hysterical parrot who'd lost his new feather.

"Never fear my brave boys, we'll beat this foul
weather. No-one hold back... We're in it together.
Fred's Sunday–best bloomers will make a fine Royal,
so haul away boys, it's worth all the toil."

The reinforced gusset took up the strain with sleet
and snow and driving hard rain.

"See those fine stitches, let it roar let it blow. In a
week I promise, we'll see old Valparaiso."

And just as he said, they arrived 'tho half dead and
begrudgingly thanking now knickerless - Fred.

Later that day the crew lined up for some advance of
their pay; and as each signed the disbursement form,
praised Ned for saving them from the terrible storm.

Next morning at breakfast Fred said, "They've all
gone!"

****

"I must have a cook."
Said Ned to the agent – who directed him to a place
called 'The Stable'. An infamous pub, well known for
bad grub but girls who were willing and able.
There he met Mabel. She had lost all her glam, was
missing some teeth and her varicose veins made
her testy... but her C.V. was impressive... and she

made a very fine pasty. Hard to believe, she'd once been 'The Queen': South America's famous 'Loving Machine'.

"I want you away in a month, and not a day longer." The shipper had firmly asserted. A problem for Ned and he shook his head, for the crew had mostly deserted.
The boarding house crimps, the crooks and the pimps would find him the maritime dregs, but you had to be fit, loading a ship: eighteen hundred tons of stinking old… guano!

Saddest of all that troubled Ned and filled him with tearful emotion. The space in his bed was missing big Fred, his reliable trustworthy bosun.
It's in prison she'll stay, for many a day for killing a Swede in a brawl – It was said he provoked her bad temper; but the judge would not listen and ten years in the dock he has sent her.
She has left him her bloomers for a spare topmast sail and of his good nature she did further prevail and asked him to care for her parrot.

"And when you're at sea, just think of me when you look at my bald-headed friend. No letters dear Ned, I've said all I've said… take care of my parrot and call him 'Young Fred'."

The cabin boy returned – love lessons learned, tho' Maria said she'd "Always love him."

Then the cash ran out and so did Maria – straight
into the arms of a new, richer, sailor.

The crew shortage was solved by a man called
Abdul… who fitted a steam **donkey** engine. He
wobbled his head and impressed Captain Ned with
its power to lift more than ten men could.
It cost a few bob but replaced many men; it only
needs water and firewood.

In no time at all they were loaded and full – and the
old 'CROSS-EYED RAVEN' steered into the ocean.
The drunks they all cheered for missing that berth
– and they bet their last dollar… she's never reach
Perth.

****

What To Do With A Didgeridoo?

Despite others convictions and clear dereliction – the old *"CROSS-EYED RAVEN"* kept steadily on course.

Ned studied the chart with the navigator's art and calculated the best weather slot.
There was no hurry, or record to steal, with three feet of weed hanging down under the keel… they'll barely make four knots.

A passage ahead of the long boring kind; Ned guessed there'd be some with trouble in mind. So he knew he was right, with a bit of foresight to sell the upright piano.
With a set of new sails and bags of 'top soil', to mix with a bit of the guano… he'd start a *GARDENING CLUB*!

The cook was pleased with carrots and peas, big runner beans; great aubergines and dozens of giant cucumbers. Pansies in the fo'c'sle, trees up on the poop; leeks growing in fire buckets… melons in the coup.
And happy chickens, pecking up to their arse on number two hatch, now covered in grass.
So everyone ate well and hearty and all joking aside – tho'some did deride –it was down to the captain's initiative… Until a wave swept it all over the side!

Young Fred the parrot with a much better lifestyle,

grew a set of handsome new feathers; but with grim determination refused to improve on his lower deck manners.

****

Finally they sighted Perth up ahead, rising out of the morning mist – and very soon the pilot boarded with a lengthy medicine list.

"Cap'n Blue, I implore of you, to search your medicine chest. To cure the drip that hangs off my nose; the fungal infection between my toes… and an embarrassing private itch."

"The doctor in Perth has banned me from seeking his attention; for I drank all his potions and other things… I dare not mention."

It made Ned think – for the man has a problem with drink. But when he finally agreed to waive pilot fees – and putting her secure fore and aft… Ned paid the dues that was asked… with a pint of the dreaded 'Black-draught'!

****

Opening the hatch the sky turned black with a cloud of stowaway flies… and the terrible stink made the dock-workers blink – demanding extra for watery eyes.

Ned heard the roar and as his feet touched the floor

he was confronted by an angry Australian boss stevedore.

"I say there Mate – we need a debate about a load of shy... which falls from great height upon the heads of my men. Up in the cross-trees, pooping with ease... a bloody great speckled HEN!
And if you don't put it right we're all out on strike... Mate!"

Ned glowered.

"Firstly Mate – I'm not the mate. He's the mate, the one with gold bands to whom your complaint should relate. I'm the captain and don't you forget."

"As for the chicken: She's very upset; she flew up into the trees on the night all her friends got washed over the side. She's refusing to leave... unless you can think of a tempting bribe?"

****

In the end: Not a bad trip, but too many requesting to see the port doctor. The usual trick, claiming sick... an excuse to get to the boozer.

Ned wrote them their notes. Beginning with seaman Jack Flynn; genuinely hurt with his arm in a sling. One on cheap wooden crutches; three with V.D. and one with strange purple rashes.
Another gone mad, or so he pretended but was gone like a shot, when the trip ended.

Doctor Jack – a popular chap famously known for his tonic and patented sterilizer… one part water, three parts gin and a double scotch for reviver.

First in line, feeling otherwise fine was a worried young Michael Lee… who had a troubling 'lump'.

"Drop yer trews." (Said the doctor.) Fer my diagnosis… Make a good cough… Let's see them jump… They look a bit red."

"But doc are you sure? The problem I've got is a lump n my **head**"

Not so lucky was Jimmy Malloy; the tall and skinny, young cabin boy.
Doctor Jack was in great form, and with his own invention of green chloroform – removed his tonsils and big toe nail.
A lot of trouble for him to make… The boy only went in with a nagging toothache.

****

The cargo discharged and time to move and now a few things for Ned to prove, if going to land a profitable charter.

First. Up on the grid-iron and scrape off the barnacles, the weed and the slime. Paint her bottom with a coat of white lead for the speed she would need on the trip up ahead.
The crew didn't like it, covered in paint and blisters

from scraping and painting in the terrible heat.

"Yer not to leave till it's finished!"
The bosun had said; then sneaked off for a smoke in
the loo.
They wanted revenge: and when he was gone,
judging the moment just right... with a brush on a
stick, up the crew's toilet pipe... they painted his bum
letter-box red.

****

Captain Ned was in luck; for a ship was stuck, on the
rocks just beyond the pilotage range. And he put in a
price that turned out just right, to take her cargo and
passengers to New Zealand.

Next morning some bawling and commotion from the
crew's fo'c'sle head. A man refusing to get out of bed.
The bosun said, "You're really not trying"
The bloke replied, "Bugger off – I think I'm dying!"

The bosun reported to the cocky second mate.
"A bloke in the fo'c'sle, I'd like you to see... I reckon
he's taking the 'P' out of me... He said in the night he
went to the dunny and got bitten by a bloody great
flea?"

The stevedore standing nearby, let out a cry.
"S'truth Mate – I hope yer not too late – those things
don't 'ave to be bigger. Sounds ta me: it ain't a flea,
but the deadly little 'Black 'Widda'"

"Get lost! Nobody gets seriously bit by a spider."
The second mate said.
Next morning – the poor bloke was dead!

****

The Second Mate Andy, not very popular, sarcastic
and bandy. High testosterone levels and constantly
randy. With every opportunity or any excuse he'd
seek women out to try to seduce – And kept a score
card of women he'd laid… it was all lies of course, for
most he had paid.
He went after Doctor Jack's nurse Rose – to whom
he proposed; which was part of his usual technique.
But she found him too weak, his efforts too slight…
preferring young men who'd keep going all night!
The romance suddenly came to an end. Returning
Rose home late at night, in the dark, a little bit tight…
The house wasn't right.
Andy pushed her through the skylight window…
knocking old Mrs. Miles, attending her piles, clean off
the loo.
In a terrible state she called the police and
demanded Andy's arrest. And next time, the judge
warned him of what he might get, for showing women
such little respect.

The passengers boarded later that day; a miner, a
colonel and his niece and four nuns requiring a cabin
a-piece.
No tip for Jimmy Malloy **this** trip.

The agent came aboard with Ned's sailing orders;

and a long sack-wrapped object tied up at the corners.
"No problems Cap' that I can see… maybe a bit bumpy in the Tasman Sea. Apart from that it shouldn't take you long to reach the port of Welling**ton**."

Then he hesitated.
"A little extra Cap' and a bonus for you… something else I'd like you to do. Instead of calling in to Tasmania and all that entails. You are requested to carry this… a most valuable didgeridoo. Just pass it over the rails."

Ned looked stern and quizzical.
"It's a strange request you have for me, discharging cargo whilst moving at sea?"

The agent coughed and made a wink.
"It avoids all the trouble and cost of a berth, and duty paid to custom officials. Off Flinders Island in the Bass Strait a fast boat will meet you either early or late… You will only be required to sign your initials."
"Bon voyage Captain!"

****

At sea that night in the cosy saloon, they squeezed around the table, with just enough room – of which the colonel soon complained.

"With my gout – tight situations give me great pain."

They all squeezed up a little more and the miner
ended up flat on the saloon floor.
Felicity the colonel's niece, thought this funny and
she laughed with child-like glee… at the same time
suggestively squeezing… the captain's left knee.
Ned stood up.

"I welcome you aboard one and all, to my old ship
and I hope we will have a comfortable trip. Use all
the deck space and feel quite free… It'll help time
pass whilst at sea."

He raised a glass of Bordeaux red – The nuns all
frowned.

"Young man – grace has not been said."

"Here's to a safe trip. And for dinner tonight – we've a
huge roast hen for your delight."

****

"I dunno." Ned said to Young Fred, as he sat that
night on the edge of his bed.

"Strange old country this one… strange things too.
A thing like a dog with great big feet…more than ten
feet they say it can leap… called a kangaroo. And
now a precious long stick with a hole in the middle –
they call a didgeridoo."

****

Bounding along the Australian Bight, the seas on the beam, the wind just right.
And the passengers settling in very well, despite the rolling from the S'ly swell.

And Felicity, Janet Blenkinsop was running around having a great time, teasing the crew, keeping the bosun in line. She's having fun with the second mate; flirting cruelly and boosting his ego; encouraging stories of the women he's had; he chasing her like a bandy old crab…

But she had her eyes on another prize.

Billy the miner is missing his shovel and pick, hating the sea; he stays in bed always seasick.

And the colonel looks for trouble and constantly complains despite all the port to drown his gout pains.

****

On a pleasant afternoon, the guests having left the dining saloon. Young Fred and Ned decided to examine the package stowed under his bed.
The wrapping removed, the wood smooth and exposed. Ned never heard Felicity enter…on her tip toes.

"**My Ned**," She said, "That's a big one; a shame though you have nothing better to do, than huff and puff on an old didgeridoo."

She gave a suggestive smile, then jumped up on
his bed, throwing back the covers and exposing the
bows, on her long, pink knickers.

"Captain... it's not fair." She purred.
"Your bed's much bigger than the others."

With an ache in his groin and deepening breath,
he knew he was experiencing one of man's biggest
tests.
A disciplined captain, in full control - or a red-blooded
sailor, game for a 'pull'.
And as he drew closer, 'heaven' at arm's reach...
Fred just let go, with a blood-curdling screech.
That killed the passion and Felicity was gone. She
swung Fred a punch, which he easily avoided as he
escorted her out.
And the nuns who were reading beside the spud pen,
awarded Felicity 'For feminine prowess': three points
out of ten.

Ned persisted; he was determined to try- and play
that old didgeridoo. In addition to helping time to
pass by... it was something new, something to do.

He huffed and he puffed; red faced and cross eyed,
not a sound emerged, as hard as he tried/
Young Fred jumped down from the swing on his
perch.

"I think it's time for a little <u>re</u>search."

He looked in the small end; walked up and down its

full length, then without fearing – into the big end, his
tail disappearing.
Ned called out:

"Fred. If you get stuck, I can't get you out."

Then with a scratching and cursing Fred re-emerged
– dragging a waxed linen parcel, carefully sealed.
Ned cut it open, stitch by stitch, until its contents
revealed…

"S'truth Fred… We're going to be rich!"
………..**Ten dazzling diamonds**………..

****

"Flinders Island – fine on the bow!"

The lookout called from up on the prow.
Ned gritted his teeth, (a warning sign), to the men
that would trick him – a party to crime.

They sped alongside, and didn't hide, the guns
trained on the steering position, from their port side.
The parcel slid over to four eager hands, then pulled
away quickly – the end of their mission.
Or so they thought!

Ned, helm down, shouted, "Let's go!"
For locked in his cabin, something no-one should
know.

He had hoped to slip away in the gathering dark but

now the scene became a little concerning... coming
up behind, bow wave churning... the sloop was
returning.

He guessed they'd unwrapped their valuable
package – and didn't like the words, used in his
message.
They pulled alongside – again all guns trained.

"Where is our package? You'd best send it down...
You've got just ten seconds or we'll board, and
mister... you're going to drown."

Ned ordered everyone but the bosun, below. Then
grabbed the helm and put it hard over – shouting...

"This is the way – we're going to go!"

The ships collided, the sloop pulling ahead, until she
was positioned under 'Raven's' wide fo'c'sle head.
The bosun had crept forward, sharp knife in hand,
and when Ned shouted "NOW" cut the tight lashing
bands:... of the starboard anchor, which weighed a
few tons – now crashing down, unable to stop her –
clean through the sloop... to Davey Jones locker.

They pulled away into the red end of the day and in
minutes the sloop disappeared and Ned feared there
was nothing he could do. All that remained floating,
some bits of wreckage... and a didgeridoo.

****

Back in his cabin, in his hand a large brandy. He opened the double locked drawer – to look at the cause of all this trouble; he'd report to the customs in Wellington…
But the package was gone!!

****

Ned and the mate searched the ship end to end, tip to tip… but no valuable package…It had been nicked!

They stripped the crew, the passengers too – except the ladies of course.
The colonel thought he was back on duty and joined in what he thought was fun, lifting Fred's tail – to search up his bum.
Fred said loudly… "F**K OFF"… The feathers standing up on the back of his head… he was no hen. The nuns were impressed and scored him nine out of ten.

They searched again, to check and re-check – catching Felicity snogging the second mate on the orlop deck: But nothing!

****

Once in port and the police on board, they didn't believe the story Ned told… and so arrested him.

But before they locked him up for the night, the agent arrived…

"Good news Mate – you'll be alright. I've just heard the news, you wouldn't believe… running down the old Main Street, like frightened grey rabbits. Four nun imposters were caught… with diamonds sewn into their habits!"

****

Abdul's Amazing Steam Machine

Wellington was fine and Ned had a great time
enjoying good food and drinking wine and in the
casino he'd had some fun, betting and winning
somebody's gun.

But now the holds are fairly full with a cargo of New
Zealand's finest wool – bound for Bristol, their first
port of call.

Ned has secured a very good price for an additional
cargo of Asian spice, which on the day could double
his pay; for once again reliably told, as tastes
improve, just like tea... worth more than gold!

So they are bound for Makassa in the Flores Sea
and on the way for a bit **more** pay, to divert to
Vanu Levu in the Fiji isles – to embark an important
dignitary.

****

Passengers are three: The colonel and niece Felicity;
and a strange Chinese lady Mrs. Min. Tall and thin;
not too bad with her false teeth in...but get up close,
her breath is gross and stubble grows out of her chin.
The cabin boy Jimmy is not very happy when
ordered by her.

"Go get my bags and make it snappy!"

And for his efforts she tipped him a farthing. But then demanded it back with a vitriolic attack:-

"My cabin's not right – the bed's too tight
And a cockroach gave me a terrible fright
Running around my hand wash basin."

The crew have bought a pet snake called Victor, a friendly little boa constrictor; whose job it is to eat rats and mice and although they're not very nice – cockroaches.

But he's a lazy snake, spending most of his time curled up in bed... dreaming of ways to ambush Young Fred – for vermin aside, his favourite dish is freshly pressed young parrot.

****

Back at sea and running free, with the wind from a favourable direction. Ned assembled the officers to accompany him on a routine ship's inspection.

The rigging was good and the decks scrubbed clean – the brass all shiny, the best it's been. The colonel was sitting in his wicker chair.
Mrs. Min was strolling, taking in the sea air.
But of flighty Felicity – nothing's been seen.

Ned called out to the bosun aloft.
"Have you seen the girl who usually gets in your hair?"

"Aye Sir, she's gone off sulking down the stairs.
I 'ad to warn 'er good and loud – to stop climbing up
the mainmast shroud.
Exposing her bloomers to a red-blooded crew… such
distractions will not do"

****

Through the Fiji Basin. No storms or rain that could
hide a reef, which came to Ned with great relief; for
he had pushed on sail so they wouldn't be late, but
some tricky waters to navigate.

The only incident worth a mention was the day that
Victor was put on detention. Bad tempered and
grumpy and frequently hissing – he slid out of bed
and was posted 'missing'.

They searched the ship high and low; the rats and
mice knew where to go but **they** weren't telling.
And Ned grew fed up… everyone yelling… 'Victor'!

He knew alright his destination. He wanted to be
adopted by a first class client, who would suitably
improve his fo'c'sle diet.
So at the right moment he slipped into Felicity's
bed…and snuggled up close.
A smile spread slowly across her face and she
dreamt of a past love, Eric.
But when she discovered it was three feet long, she
had a fit of hysterics.

****

They navigated the islands of Fiji and finally Vanu
Levu was in sight... A Garden of Eden, a tropical
delight; with palm trees down to the sea. The water
bright blue... and the pilot came out in a dugout
canoe.
He boarded just as Felicity arrived, her nightmare
abated... but it didn't last long, with the pilot almost
stark naked.
The channel was easily seen, it was clearly deeper
when the water turned emerald green.
Finally tying up on a rough wooden jetty... covered in
suitcases... and little boys fishing – a chance to stow
away, not worth missing.

The passengers turned up in a covered sedan,
attended by servants and a medicine man... who
was tall and handsome with a light brown tan, and
sarong covering bits not to mention... but clearly
caught, Felicity's attention.

Then out she stepped: Big Queen Rannapam: every
inch of her tattooed, even fingers and knuckles...
right down to her toes; a necklace of shark's teeth,
and her grandmother's finger-bone stuck through her
nose.

Next to emerge from that mobile home... standing
alone... the most beautiful woman Ned had seen –
Lady-in-waiting to Her Majesty, the Queen.
This was Lisa – a real life copy of the Mona Lisa;
a perfect beauty of just the right size. The crew
were transfixed... the second mate stumbled...
mesmerized. Felicity was not so impressed. She

thought Lisa looked silly in her South Seas dress.

But now a few problems for them to solve: Queen Rannapam too big, the 'RAVEN'S' gangway too small...They stood in a huddle. A situation not foreseen...Do something quickly, she's an impatient queen.
Then Young Fred solved it!

"Use Abdul's wonderful **steam** machine."

Too big for a bed; so instead, the sailmaker sewed a double size hammock using super-strength thread, with perfect seams... held in each corner to the deck-head beams.

Lisa glided about, quite serene; dancing attendance on her big fat queen... who said to Ned:

"On my island I sit on a throne made of coral and marzipan – which I constantly eat, that's why I'm 25 stone. So I'm going to to Makassar to see a man who will make me a throne of inlaid ivory and polished stone."

The ship secure and ready to go. Abdul's engine still aglow and quietly hissing. Reported to Ned:

"Someone's missing." ...Mrs. Min!

Last seen talking to the skipper of a high speed outrigged canoe.

"This won't do and if she's not here soon I'll leave her behind. There's only an hour to catch the tide."

She suddenly turned up, averting her eyes. She'd bought a wide brimmed hat of an unlikely size... sporting a peacock's feather?

They sailed away just in time, the sun setting into a sea of blue and lime.
But gone was the strong easterly wind, replaced with a variable, gentle breeze. Not what Ned wanted – for this long trip into the Coral Sea; for a ship this size handles better when she's all, running-free.
And what all sailors dread:
To be caught on a lee shore... so be wary of places not travelled before.

They crossed the top of Australia, through the Torres **Strait** and on into the Arafura Sea – but for the right kind of wind... they were again too late.

****

The '*CROSS-EYED RAVEN*' rolled gently to the ocean swell. The chickens were laying, the pigs are well – though something is troubling the captain; something even **he** was unable to tell.

Abdul's boiler maintained a full head of steam, to position the sedan for the Island Queen...for she liked the view just right: A remarkable piece of lucky foresight.
And she liked her tea at ten past three!

Ned came on deck; last check that night.

The helmsman turned the wheel a notch…eight bells struck, the end of the watch.
Casting an eye at the state of the sea, came to rest on the starboard lee… and from the shadows he could only stare at the vision of loveliness standing there.
A long silk sarong, white flower in her hair, staring out to sea… wistfully.

Beside Abdul's boiler, still gently hissing, he thought of things that he'd been missing… a gentle caress… female kissing.

He turned his thoughts back to the nautical kind – important things he had in mind.
To steer a course across the Arafura Sea, as clear of islands as he could get – for reefs apart, they posed **another** threat?
But even he couldn't deny that as of late, he was having trouble to concentrate… on every surface he could see her, the sweetly, smiling face of Lisa.
Then it happened!!
Next morning. Preparing for breakfast, a little late. In the mirror looking back – an unshaven chin; hair not combed; collar worn thin. Things that normally did not matter. Now… all of a sudden Ned. Heavens above, I think you're in **love**!

That night, under a star filled sky; the beautiful Lisa caught Ned's eye. Our captain not being the romantic kind, summoned all the courage that he could find…

he must not fail... walked over and joined her at the leeward rail.

She turned and smiled which made him glow; and without hesitation he said:-

"Lisa – please don't be offended.
I have something to say. I want you to know, I am a hard-working man and always do my duty.
And women I have met, but none to match **your** beauty.
I thought I had everything I could want in this life, but now I realise... it's missing a wife.
I'm sorry it's sudden but I no longer can hide – the need to ask you...to be my bride?"

She turned and pressed a finger across his lips and looking up with her big brown eyes, her chest heaved and she sobbed with pitiful sighs.

"Thank you Ned for your compliment. I know you would make me most content. And I couldn't imagine a better life, than being yours... a captain's wife.
But it just cannot be our plan... for I am promised to **another** man."

He dried the tears that she freely wept. His heart now heavy with loss and regret. And she continued through heart-felt sobs:-

"Oh Ned I will miss your lovely smile and all your kind attention.
But in the time of things it is but for a little while.
Between our cultures please don't let there be a wedge...and understand: We would rather die than

break a pledge."

****

Next afternoon, feeling down-hearted; knowing he and the love of his life, soon to be parted. A boy from aloft, being taught sailors know-how.

"A sail to starboard – four points on the bow!"

Alone on the ocean sometimes weeks on end – it's always good to meet a friend. For that's what they are, one to another – a common cause, maritime brother.
But not always!

Ned steadied the telescope on the shining horizon. A red sailed junk about its business or something else… a bit more serious?

Only zephyr-like winds scudded over the sea. The junk being lighter manoeuvred more easily… moving slowly up, under their lee.

The image he could now make out much clearer. A flag went up 'I AM IN DISTRESS' as the craft drew nearer.

Instinct made Ned tense –was this genuine or… the island threat of the infamous Malay pirates bold? Be **most** vigilant he had been told.
But first and foremost he had a duty that all seamen respect. To do their best to help others… when in

distress.

Now Young Fred sensed a reason for caution… a memory fixed as a fledgling, when he was stolen and sold at auction.
He made a noise like a demented rattle.

"Shut up." Said Ned. "Stop your prattle."

Naked bodies stretched across the hatch boards.
Are they exhausted.., or hiding swords?

Ned called over to Abdul.

"We've possibly patients to lift aboard. So flash up your boiler …food and water we can afford."

And then, too late: The moment he caught sight, flying from her masthead… in the bright sunlight **Peacock Feathers**!

As he shouted a general warning, the pirates already were swarming… up ropes and ladders; a grapnel landing in Queen Rannapam's awning.

"Gather aft as quick as you can; grab any weapon, a knife, a spike, the cook's frying pan!"

But now the heathen were pouring aboard, screaming like banshees – an evil horde.

The colonel unable to move from his old wicker chair, withdrew a sword which he waved in the air. (Where did he get **that** from?) And when a pirate kicked his gout, he landed him a deadly clout.

Queen Rannapam got into a state, shouting repeatedly,

"Pillage and Rape!"

But never-the-less with indignant rage, leapt into the air and squashed four of them flat.

All hands were now pressed down by the poop.

"Get below." Ned said to the mate, handing the keys. "We're in for some fun; go to my cabin, get my gun."

But they were too late.
The mate stepped back from behind the door – a musket pressed up under his chin… closely followed by Mrs. Min!

The stinking horde pressed closer. Leg-irons clinking, weapons glinting… And Ned could tell by the look in their eyes, Lisa would be their number one prize.
So he grabbed the nearest thing to him – a lignum-vitae belaying pin… and cracked the first one over the head. The next was quickly at him, his rapier catching Ned's shoulder; but he never got the chance to be bolder and the price he paid for his pirating sin, was a deadly blow from Ned's wooden pin.

The colonel swung his sword wildly in the air; an old Hussar, more used to horse-back than a wicker chair.

He sliced one in passing and caught the next in line
– he's back on the battlefield, having a **wonderful**
time…

Now Victor (the secret weapon) only three feet long,
he never-the-less was very strong… despite 'Lazy
long worm' as he'd been branded – strangled three
pirates single handed!

But odds were against them, they were losing the
fight – a man grabbed a terrified Lisa and Ned ended
his life… the crowd all grew silent… for an incredible
sight.

Swinging over the bulwark, elegant and tall; a
swash-buckling adventurer stood over them all.
Dark, handsome features, black hair tied in a neat
pony tail; long tapered fingers and manicured nails;
tight fitting shirt, lace cuffs and collar. A pencil
moustache; tight-fitting breeches with long boots to
match.
And with hands on hips:-

"My name is Barabbas, scourge of the South China
Seas. I've been chasing you for **ages**, since our first
sighting.
It's a shame you resisted, but now let's stop all this
fighting. We are too many, and you cannot win. I hate
all this violence."

He said with a grin.

And then he turned to Mrs. Min.

"Mother! – And you've got me a hat; you kept your promise, I'll look good in that."

But mother love was not on the plate.

"About time **too** – you are **very** late. My bags are stowed in the cabin below, get down and fill them – I'm ready to go."

Captain Ned's teeth gritted – it appeared there was no choice; surprised as he was by Barabbas, squeaky, high-pitched voice.
And Young Fred whispered into his left ear.

"I do believe he's a little bit...peculiar?"

Felicity, hearing the commotion ran on deck – answers to seek ...took one look at Barabbas, he legs turned all jelly and weak.

Another lunged at Lisa and despite a knife to his throat, Ned's knee came up like a rocket ...right in the 'old John-'o'-groats'!

Barabbas turned and went below to seek out the valuable plunder. And the pirates hauled up leg-irons, the tools of their pirating vice ...Apart from the cargo – slaves fetch a very good price.

Felicity frightened/excited; her hormones confused ... put on a most convincing ruse.

"I must go below and powder my nose."

She could hear his movements – her heart was pounding
…was she daring or being a fool? They never taught this at finishing school.
Into her cabin and she was in for a shock …the pirate captain was wearing one of her frocks?

"I like this one." He said with a twirl …In front of a mirror - just like a girl.

And spread out on her bed, a selection in red …
dresses, petticoats and bloomers.
He was now wearing her see-through pyjamas.

Felicity confused and not amused, swept the clothes from her bed and completely lost her temper.

"Oh for **goodness sake** – let's get on with the rape. I really won't mind – in fact, I'd be elated.
I have been very frustrated …and I guess you are the experienced kind?
So let me get ready – but please be steady with your seafaring versions …I'm a church-going girl and not into perversions."

Barabbas stepped back in horror.

"I am **sorry** young lady: I'm a very poor version of the masculine person which is clearly your fantasy.
I just love frocks and playing with dollies …and prefer to sit down for a pee!"

Back on deck Ned and Abdul had worked out a plan.

Leaving the crew in a group he inched forward, a club in his hand. The pirates suspicious, followed his move …around the fo'c'sle, stopped at the crews loo.

"**NOW!**" He shouted.

Abdul appeared all covered in soot – his eyes peering out, a frightening look …and the pirates all jumped up into the air and screamed …For Abdul had opened the valve to the steam.
The cloud soon enveloped them, a strange shade of green?

"Use the confusion and grab all their weapons …
there's swords and some guns – quite a selection."

And in no time at all the crew had them pinned to the wall just under the fo'c'sle-head steps. The pirates now wailing with panic and scalds …full of regrets.

Barabbas reappeared upon the deck – hands on hips, puckered lips.

"Call yourselves **Pirates** – you're a bunch of nits; all this yelling and pretending – gets on my tits!"

"I surrender captain …I am all yours. But don't let your men touch me with their grubby paws.
I'm fed up with marauding; I much prefer clothes to old dirty swords and soft woollen carpets to salty deck boards.
It's all my old dad's fault: Called himself 'Satan The Pirate King' and wanted a son to follow him.

But my younger brother was stronger and fitter – I'm
a disappointment …just ask my mother.
So take me captain – lock me in your first class
dungeon …I just cannot wait to go shopping in
London."
"You stupid fool." Ned replied with contempt. "Do you
really believe I would relent, for the filthy trade **you**
represent.
If I take you to Makassar you will surely hang, but
lucky for you I've **another** plan.
You and your crew I cannot water and feed …I have
no choice, you're going to be freed. But with only one
sail and your basic needs. It is all that I can do. **But**,
for a change, before we go, my crew just cannot wait
…to plunder **you**!"

Throughout the fight Fred had been sitting, on Ned's
shoulder, very tight and just as Barabbus said his
goodbyes, Fred delivered an enormous splat – just
missed his eyes.

The dust all settled – the junk out of sight; blood
washed away; whisky all-round easily afforded – the
crew all cheerful and well rewarded.
Then someone said:-

"The colonel is dead."

They looked for wounds, he'd taken some flak, but
finally concluded …a heart attack!
Before sunset, before the crew were fed; our noble
captain with respect for the dead – a funeral service
from the Bible was read.

And at the tenderest moment from the back of the
crowd – someone farted – rather loud.
Ned was annoyed.
"To you who farted, just show more respect for the
recently departed."

If Young Fred could blush …he **would**!

****

Later that night, sat in his cabin; a brandy to hand,
going over the dramas of that pirate band.
Timbers creaking – a gentle sigh of the wind; soft
glow from the oil lamp, Young Fred having a doze …
when a familiar perfume drifted into his nose.
As quiet as the night she had entered his room;
her hair on her shoulder, the flower removed and a
simple white shift…her sweet mystery increased.

"Although the pledge I still must keep. And for what
might have been I will secretly weep.
I know that I owe you my life …and for one night will
be your wife …if that is what **you** would like?"

And she kissed the wound on his shoulder.
For Young Fred, a moment so tender, even he had a
tear in his eye …Then the sheet was pulled over his
cage!!

****

The wind picked up and they moved a lot faster and
very soon reached the port of Makassar.

A brief farewell on the gangway – hands parted,
a feeling of emptiness as she passed; Queen
Rannapam gave Ned a knowing wink.

Cargo loaded, food and water aboard. The crew with
hangovers having spent some of their hoard.
Our Ned heavy-hearted will control his emotion – as
they face the last leg and the Indian Ocean.

She pushed along with her bowsprit dipping into the
swell and will reach the Cape of Good Hope, very
soon; helped along by a fresh **monsoon.**
Not much news for the log to relate, except an area
of ocean – mile upon mile, brown with sea snakes.
And flying fish suppers the cook served just right –
replenished daily, they flew aboard every night.

Off the Portuguese coast Ned had quite a shock – he
felt a great 'thump', made the fo'c'sle bell rock.
A great sperm whale, recognising the *'RAVEN'*
as once being a Whaler and Felicity on deck (not
dressed as a sailor) …it resented her corset.
Young Fred understood as only non-humans could,
the message sent out by the whale.
And typically tragic, the need for baleen …Felicity
was wearing the best there had been …in fact she
was wearing the whale's old **grandad**!

As the *'ONE-EYED RAVEN'* approached the old
Bristol quay, awaiting there to greet her, larger than
life for all to see …the barmaid Fredrika!

In Santiago she put down a riot in the jail.

And the judge's decision to free her prevailed and to the docks he had provided a carriage – even tho' she'd refused his offer of marriage.
Now she's back in her dockside pub and looking for her Fred …with a chest full of love (and Brazil nuts).

With a tear in his eye he flew down to meet her. For she had loved him from being a fluffy wee chick and although for Ned he felt much love …he preferred the grub in the dockside pub.

****

Billy Boot

Back as a mate; no luck of late securing a post as a skipper.
So he set off again, for he'd heard the rumour – a position was going on a five-masted schooner.

In the dead of the night, in the wind and the rain he arrived at the port of departure.
Down a dark cobbled street, carrying his sea-going trunk, slipping and cursing – tripping over a drunk
…he could see the schooner, lying out at anchor. A handsome ship, fine lines and in very good nick – but something about her was troubling.

Ruby. The landlady of the 'Old Barley Mow' called out:

"Find time for an ale Sir? Before you must go.
Choose one of my girls, they're all very nice – The one with bad breath you can have for half price!"

Ned was feeling quite weary.

"I think you are right. I'll stop for a while, for a pie and a pint."

All cosy and warm in the dark saloon bar, which smelled of tobacco, old ale and a slight hint of tar.
The log fire flickering; cat chewing the remains of a mouse; distant fiddle and singing …a sailorman's

house.

When out of the darkness Ned got quite a fright – a
black girl appeared, she just slid out of the night.

"My name is Poppy. I hear you are mate, of the five-
masted schooner that arrived here of late. It's off
to West Africa, the mysterious Gold Coast; she's
carrying dried fish and Queen Vic's post. Now – if
you are willing, I'll pay you ten shillings to take a gift
in a box for my Nan!"

That was a lot for a mate, with a bill running up on
the slate; however …he felt he must caution.

"The West Coast's a big place, and full of your race.
I wish I could help, but try as hard as I can, it's most
unlikely I'll find your old Nan."

"Never you fear – she'll find **you** my dear …I know
how you feel but let's shake hands on the deal …and
please, not a word to big Ruby.
I'm not one of her girls; she thinks I have a strange
foreign illness. I do all the chores, look after the
whores …but mostly chambermaiding. Ruby did her
best to persuade me: "number one choice of the
crew" But the man ran off in the night screaming…
not liking my African Voodoo.

On the quay the next day awaiting the boat, in his
officer's cap and fur-lined coat. A horse and cart
turned up with poppy's box.

"S'truth," Said Ned, "That's a whopper."

The boatman was moaning, he was only a lad; the box and our Ned took all the space he had.

Ned took a deep sniff:

"Young man, you 'niff' – in fact your hygiene is most unsound."

"Not me sir, it's the cargo – dried cod from old Newfoundland; highly prized where **we** are bound."

****

The captain was tall, slim and quite elegant. A Nelsonian touch; a patch on one eye and a gold Hunter watch.
He looked up at Ned from his mahogany desk, lit a cigarette in a solid gold holder…

"I'll expect much of you; just watch out for the crew, they're scumbags and will try every trick. Be firm and careful, watch from behind – don't permit drinking, they're a mutinous kind."

Ned was a-wondering as he unpacked his sea-going bag, why the captain signed-on, such a bunch of brigands: when with good gear and comfort he could have chosen the **finest** of hands.

Out of the corner of his bloodshot left eye… Poppy's box wobbled …then fell over, the lashings let fly.

What followed gave Ned a surprise …Out stepped
Poppy – as cool as you can, wearing a wig and
dressed like a man.

"What on earth are you doing? You cannot stay here;
the captain will jail you, the crew will do worse. It's a
lot you are expecting for the cash in my purse."

"Do not fear Ned; it's all been arranged. The
steward's with Ruby, as drunk as a coot …Please
introduce me to the captain, let's say …I'm your
seafaring assistant – young Billy Boot!"

A tug towed them out and over the bar. The pilot
said, "Farewell." And whispered to Ned,

"Good luck, you might need it, she's a ship bound for
hell."

They were making good progress with a press on her
sails; a nor'westerly blowing right up her tail.
Ned was impressed with her tackle, her sails and her
speed – in all situations, a ship you would need.
The crew they were surly, but respected our Ned, for
his skills as a sailor, words need not be said.

Billy Boot as steward took care of the officers needs;
the captain impressed with his strength and his
speed. He served them meals, kept their cabins
clean and washed all their clothes…a much better
servant than ever there'd been.
Never guessing that beneath, a girl sweet and tender
– the captain quite clueless, to Billy Boot's gender.

As he feared, Ned's having trouble keeping the crew in line, despite comfortable quarters and the food being fine.
A man refused to reef a mainsail: this is considered a maritime sin. So Ned whacked him hard with the cook's rolling pin.

"Get up," Ned said to a man in his bed. "The wind is beginning to roar."

"Sod off!" Said the man…

So Ned whacked this one, with the cook's frying pan.

At six in the morning he had a close shave; a seaman let a halyard fly …catching Ned in his bloodshot left eye.
At half-past ten it happened again: A knife was dropped from above, impaling itself in the deck …It could have been curtains, aimed he was certain, as he bent over exposing his neck.

But the captain did not care …preoccupied as he was, and with a far-away stare.

"Tell me Mr. Neddy …Why, if my blood is normal and red and I've had my share of women in bed, do I find young Billy …I know it sounds silly … the sole object of my desires?
When I look at his hips, his sensuous lips and full round bottom …I begin to fear I'm turning queer …I just might hit the bottle."

"Well sir, he looks normal to me and I cannot see what you are getting at …although I agree, he may be – just a little effeminate."

****

They steered south east off Senegal, then left into the Bight of Benin …on to Nigeria, but not too far, finally anchoring on the old Bonny bar.

The officials they boarded and with her papers very pleased; they took the mail and presents and without question collected their harbour fees.

Later the ship proceeded into a swampy, tree-lined creek, where normal ships don't venture; too hot to work or sleep.
Shadows soon enfolded them.
The crew rowed two longboats, to a secret wooden jetty, where they hung strange nets and secured the mooring ropes.

"A lot of trouble for some old dried fish?" Said Ned unto the captain.

"Ah, you'll be surprised, it's highly prized …and refrigeration's not been invented!"

Men, almost naked appeared out of the gloom and an entourage followed the captain to his polished saloon – four men carrying the tribal queen, in an ivory chair …a sight to be seen.

"**Steward**!" Called the captain, "Where is that man? I need drinks for my guests, please find him, as quick as you can."

But Billy had just disappeared!

Later that night she again, gave Ned a fright, appearing out of the dark. Her eyes open wide for a 'truth', she just couldn't hide:

"That old **queen** …that's my **NAN**!
She's a most wicked person, will do anything for gain, regardless of the suffering, heartache and pain. She sold me to the captain of a Portuguese slaver – to sleep in his bed …as simply a favour: And for that I promise, I'll have my revenge!"

"I know what she's up to, with her heart made of stone. I must move quickly, so please help me …I cannot do it alone."

"Do WHAT? Said Ned, "I want no part in politics or slaving."

She went through the plan over and over again – and the details made Ned's pulse quicken …to do things he'd never believe. But Poppy insisted:-

"Stick to the list and **never forget**, the old girl has this irrational fear of …CHICKENS!?"

The captain was drinking in a happy, dazed state. The crew they were missing, Poppy feared they may be too late.

'Running through the jungle, feeling like a prat –
feathers in his waistcoat, a large wattle on his cap.'

They came across a clearing.
The queen was celebrating, partying into the night.

So, now dressed just like a cockerel, his face painted
ghostly white, screaming like a banshee, Ned put
them all to fright.
The queen, with crocodile teeth and medallions, a
lion's mane upon her head; leapt at least two feet
from the cushions, on her fitted satin bed.
Her guards they had deserted their post, they'd seen
the thing they feared the most. And so without further
ado …she jumped right into the creek.
She bobbed around for a little while, then got eaten
by a crocodile.

Poppy ran into the high stockade through a creaking,
unlocked gate, but after carefully searching said:-

"I fear we are too late."

They slipped back aboard unnoticed, tho' the crew
were very near; back and celebrating on local jungle
beer. They had fulfilled their mission, the story would
unfold, the object now secure in the forward cargo
hold.

Poppy disappeared and Ned grew concerned, then
like a ghostly whisper, she silently returned …Her

eyes were full of tears.

"Those bastards have confirmed my suspicions, the
reasons for my fears.
Be careful Ned, they've got their gold, but see the
misery crammed in that stinking lower hold."

Fifty sweating, glistening bodies, looking up out of
the gloom; the whites of their eyes reflected by the
light from a cloudless moon.

From a companion door he heard a click but he'd
seen enough to feel quick sick.

They manned the oars once again and rowed out
into the ocean, but only those in number one hold
were feeling any emotion. And Poppy of course, full
of deep remorse, (for the captain aside), the truth she
just could not hide …those men were captured by
her **Grandmother's** tribe.

In the meantime Young Sid - Ned's new Parrot, had
flown off to make friends and enjoy some parrot talk
– but was back again in half an hour, fed-up with their
foreign squawk!

****

Ned studied the captain …his evil grey face: Never
should have been a member of the human race. And
before he moved to go below, Ned had a few words
he felt he should know.

"Captain Sir, I must protest: You're engaged in a trade I completely detest. There's no worse treatment this side of heaven: **Slavery** was banned back in eighty seven."

He looked at Ned through his one good eye, then let out a wearisome sigh.

"In parts of Brazil they'll look the other way, and many dollars are prepared to pay.
Just sail the ship – you'll get your dues, I'm tired of your morals, your principled views.
And I warn you again, the crew of which you are constantly complaining; the only swine that I could find, prepared for a bit of slaving.
Push them Ned, but watch your back …they'll see you dangling."

They steered due west to catch the last of the Trades, but the wind fell away in a matter of days.
The captain not happy with the ship's daily runs, and to find surprisingly north, the dreaded …
DOLDRUMS.

The crew grew idle – life becoming dull; passing time playing netball, with a sun bleached skull.
The captain now most unhappy by this stroke of fate, fearing the premium cargo, might deteriorate.
But the sky clouded over, the wind came again – the prisoners let up to get washed in the heavy tropical rain.

"I've seen the chart." Ned whispered to Poppy. "The

rendezvous he should make with ease, a hidden cove to the east of Sao Luis. But be as watchful as you can ...I doubt you and I are in the plan."

He smiled.
"Listen carefully to what I intend to do."

In the dead of night he altered course to steer for a point south of Fortaleza!

Twenty-four hours, they're closing the coast. The captain confused by the last position; now quietly enjoying a good pot roast ...Poppy keeping close and handy, his dinner accompanied with ample brandy.

Ned now strolled the listing deck ...a number of things he has to check and secretly placing a flagon of gin, close to the galley where the crew walk in.

Within half an hour as Ned expected; from the crews quarters came an increasing din ...confirming they had found the flagon of gin.

To the helmsman he said, "Go and investigate ... hurry back, don't be late." But he knew that would be the last he would see of him.

The ship was bounding along on the port tack – the lines too tight, needing some slack.

The sky pitch black, the only light from the luminous sea ...Ned swung her to starboard, quite easily.

Now they were set on her final trip a tragedy really
for this beautiful ship.

With the wind behind her, she drove like a race
horse, and Ned had a struggle keeping her on the
new course.
The captain awoke – suspicious …his pistol cocked,
but surprised to discover the door to his cabin,
securely locked …by Poppy.
Gradually through the darkness came the sound
that sailors dread, of sighing crashing breakers …
somewhere up ahead.

Ned had studied the chart carefully, he had
memorised the land …and must find the place with
gentle, sloping sand.

Poppy slipped past with a bag of gold sovereigns and
a bunch of keys, both of which she's easily relieved;
on the way locking the crew's cabin door.

"Tell them to be ready, we will run up hard. Trust
me when you leap …the water won't be deep. Then
quickly wade ashore."

He had chosen the spot with perfect aim, so they
simply climbed down the anchor chain.

But she hadn't gone: She returned to the scene and
in the light of the binnacle Ned took a deep breath…
A more **beautiful** woman he'd never seen.
Tall, shapely, a face serene. Gone were the trousers,
the wig and tight vest – now almost naked put Ned's

mind to the test! Her full rounded figure, confident smile and firm pointed breasts.

On the beach they said their "Goodbyes"; her tears he could taste, trickled from big, round eyes. Then reluctantly she pulled away from her loving, last embrace.

"Good luck my princess …forget what's been and do not hate all the white race."

They disappeared into the darkness, gold sovereigns in their hands with a beautiful queen to guide them and restore their broken pride. And in this land of opportunity …they'd form a brand new tribe. Unknown to Ned at the moment in time; when the ship came to a shuddering halt – a lantern fell over and into the gin …it caught fire! …The ship to become a funeral pyre.

But Ned didn't know. I doubt he'd care – he'd had more than enough of **them**.
With Young Sid on his shoulder and gold in his pocket, he lifted his bag …then hitched a ride to the port of Belem.

****

Warning From The Deep

In the port of Belem, Ned spent some time, looking
for a homeward berth – but he knew it might just take
a while: Not the busiest port on earth.

His pockets lined with gold sovereigns, he chose a
posh hotel; dining each day on lobster and wine and
the finest juicy steak.
And Young Sid was served Brazil nut a'-la-carte –
served on a large silver plate.

One day Ned was approached by a shipowner, a sly
and devious man; who offered him the masters job
on a barque, the "*TATTY ANNE*".

"Please sail her back to Liverpool; tho' she's not the
best you've seen, the cargo and hull are well insured
…and I know you are very keen.
She's a little bit old and cranky, and her deck has a
bit of a kink – but stuffed full of valuable logs, the old
girl's unlikely to sink."

Ned looked her over the very next day with feelings
of regret: The scruffiest ship he'd ever seen,
resembling more of a wreck.
However, it was a masters job and the voyage
shouldn't be long, but first he must find a crew …and
that was a different song.

The buck-o mate was six feet two, with a sadistic

look in his eye; woe betide the lingerer or those
who'd dare to try. He took his fun with a knotted rope
or a swift kick up the bum.

One by one they came aboard, the drunks, the
broke and retired; better men on previous ships, he'd
chased away or fired.
Except for a few Shetland Islanders, already in the
crew and they're the finest sailormen – he would trust
them through and through.

Next aboard – a bloke with a surfing board ...Ned
was most intrigued.

"I think you've got the wrong ship, mate – we're not
designed for speed!"

He stomped back down the gangway, he was really
in a huff.

"My mother's just knitted me a woollen swimsuit and
expects me to get it wet. If I return without trying it ...
she will be most upset."

Up on the deck came wee Willy McTish, carrying
his straw mattress, chipped mug and dish ...and a
separate bag containing an oversize truss?
And he walked with a suspicious limp.

Last to appear along the quay, four black horses
pulling a hearse. The gentleman in the tall black hat
showed his papers to Captain Ned, certifying that the
mummified body of a missionary, a long time now

been dead.

They only had one passenger, a Mrs. Fiona Bunting. Who said to Ned most flirtatiously, "Just call me Mrs B".

At last they were all ready for sea; the pilot booked for the evening tide.
Then a knock on the door as he settled down for a cup of tea and a kip …Four anxious Shetland Islanders.

"Cap'n. Sorry ta trouble Ye – but, we're no too happy about this trip."

"What's the problem?" Ned asked respectfully for **he** had nothing to hide.

"Tis temptin fate to sail with a body – on a Sundie … Ye must choose **another** tide."

Ned understood their suspicions and knew they'd stand on the quay. But he saw it as an omen for what might be waiting – out at sea.

****

He plotted a course to follow the old Gulf Stream which might gain a knot or two; but as for arriving in Liverpool, only a guess would do.

Mrs 'B' was everywhere, enjoying her first sea trip. Insisting on holding the timing glass as the knotted

line ran over the taff rail lip.
But now she's annoying Captain Ned: She's trying to
feminize his ship!
Tassels and folded curtains appeared on the crew's
portholes. With lavender bags and dried pressed
flowers hanging in their functional loos. Thick sliced
bread was replaced with rolls. Cloths appeared on
the table with monogrammed 'Him' and 'You'.

It really was too much!

Young Sid made a terrible fuss when she made him
a cute neck tie – but changed her mind about the
striped waistcoat ...she'd seen the look in his eye.
And she thought that his words and attitude would
be **much** more reserved. Later she complained to
Captain Ned:-

"Your parrot has snipped my specs in half and swore
with disgusting words."

****

On the latitude of Cape Hatteras the barometer
began to fall, and Ned's jaw muscles twitched ...'Not
a good place at-all!'

At the end of the day, the wind came away and blew
hard from the Sou Sou East. And Ned could tell from
the increasing swell ...it wasn't just going to pass.

The crew had reefed the mainsails and the mate was
enjoying himself, but by half-past three, even he, was

beginning to take it seriously.

With just flying jib and top sails set, Ned held her as best as he could, but the captain and crew were all aware …she was full of worm-rot wood.

At six next day the jib carried away and a split ran up the foremast. And the mate began to say his prayers: The missionary's convert at last.

Ned anxiously looked aloft as the wind began to roar, when out on deck stepped wee Willy McTish – looking a bit forlorn …Well he **would** be, in the cold and wet, as naked as the day he was born!

"What the hell d'yer think you are doing?" Ned angrily asked. And the crew began to laugh, at Willy's great swollen hernia swinging in the Atlantic draught.

"Tis something we do where I come from and you find it usually works. Wave it to old King Neptune and he'll award you storm-force points."

Willy stood up on the bulwark and his simple challenge began. Then up shot a deep green curling wave …and Willy, he was gone.

****

Each day her course set more easterly and the weather began to improve. And the crew were employed with make and mend, she couldn't have taken much more.

Mrs 'B' was nursing a cut finger and Young Sid was
making a racket – he'd just shown his opinion of her
idea – his little, fitted life-jacket.

Ned sighted Ireland's Mizzen Head …it was then the
fog set in.

Creeping along, she looked all drab and rust
streaked from her metal fittings. And strange, the
eyes in "*TATTY ANNE'S*" figurehead, the only thing
to glisten?
But that was the least of the captain's worries – he
really needed a reliable position.

Straining ears and eyes and only the hand lead-line,
they were at the mercy of currents and tides …there
was no other sign.
Then somewhere in the Irish Sea, they finally came
to grief – the keel it struck a pointed rock, known
locally as Paddy's Reef.

****

They got washed ashore in Anglesey – Ned, Young
Sid and Mrs 'B' - astride a twenty foot log.
And the four Shetland Islanders paddled into
Liverpool Bay on a buoyant, mummified body!

****

The Magnificent Art

Captain Ned, back on the beach for these are very
hard times – and the best of commands are now out
of reach, in those famous **shipping** lines.

So it's back to London docks, and the dark shady
streets of old Rotherhithe, where ladies of the night
hang out and robbers ply and hide.
To a sailors' pub:-
Well known for finding work when everything else
has failed – or for getting blind drunk when your ship
has sunk and the memory of loved-ones parted.
Only then would you consider going to 'Ye Olde Pig
Pen' – not a place for the shy or faint-hearted.

Ned opened the door and was greeted by an
odiferous roar from sailors of every nation; and
squeezed in by the bar nearest the door – best for
quick disembarkation.

Dolly the barmaid with the obligatory large chest,
tattooed arm muscles and riot-stick – no less.
A toothless comb stuck in her hair, and blackened
teeth – exposed with her grin …said to Ned.

"I guess it's gin? You're not the type to drink cheap
beer – so what on earth brings **you** in here?"

"An unlikely place to find a command; but any
officer's berth I will consider …A steamer, a sailer –

even a large coastal lugger."

"You just might be in luck. For only yesterday I beat
a first mate who refused to pay; for his tart and his
beer. I banged him on the head ...he is half dead – I
fear."

In the West India dock on cargo strewn wharves he
came up to a weary old clipper. A hard driving ship,
well rigged and equipped ...and a name that just
didn't fit her. *"MAGNIFICENT ART"*
Later he would learn, it gave the captain concern –
named for those who had charted the great seas.
But ignorant young men had defaced the great name
...adding an 'F' between the 'T' and the 'A'...

Captain Felix was fine and as Ned, once a member
of a good shipping line.
He puffed on a huge Meerschaum pipe and spoke
from a good height, for he was seven feet tall.

"Nice to have you Mr Neddy aboard this old girl and I
can tell from your papers we will get along well.
Tough it must be, for those at sea, to lose a job as
master; but I will appreciate having you as my Mate
...we will sail better and faster."

Ned smiled; for the man he admired in his
immaculate uniform coat, and waistcoat bespoke –
fine moustache and white goatee beard. A man to
respect - more than be feared.

****

On a grey summers day the ship pulled away, towed
by a big paddle tug; all covered in soot so easily
mistook … the dock master duly reported:
"The "*MAGNIFICENT FART*" has departed!"

Down the Channel and it was a fact that the ship
better known as the "*ART*" – would sail like a dream,
her bottom all clean. So a tragedy for all – the best
cargo to call – into Cardiff: a full load of **coal**!

"Yes a tragedy Ned, the best can be found for this old
girl – an Ocean Greyhound!
A cargo of coal just doesn't fit her – when you think
she was once, a famous Tea Clipper."

Ned, his jaw hard set.

"I hear what you say, but we're not finished yet."

"The French have dug a canal, which cuts weeks off
rounding The Cape. But to get anywhere at-all – the
steamers need coal …and if waiting, will just make
them late.
So ships in great numbers take coal for their bunkers
but as you and I know …steamers tend to be slow
and we can still leave them behind in our wake."

****

They lay out at anchor awaiting a berth, and the
passengers rowed out to claim the best cabins –
for these ships are cheaper and a bargain – worth
having.

Cardiff once a beautiful town, now a city all grey and brown. Covered in dust - from 'Black Diamond' it's called. COAL is the winner and steam must afford.

Dai Griffith the Chandler arrived with his cart.
"I've stores a-plenty for the "MAGNIFICENT ART."
Fresh green veg. and a ton of spuds. Oats, flour and beans - some ham …all kinds of grub. On the hoof: two pigs, ten hens, and a couple of goats thrown in."

As the coal poured aboard no breeze to relieve and dust crept around each corner and crack. And the passengers were advised to cover their clothes, to prevent them turning black.
Her once white sails, the crew will adjust – but stained forever, in Welsh coal dust.

****

Battening down and preparing for sea the carpenter hammered in hatch wedges, to secure tarpaulins; livestock pens and tethers – always prepared for the foulest of weather.
He carried on hammering awkwardly…and Ned wondered why? Then slowly began to realise, that despite the great big fluffy beard …nothing changes deep, shifty black eyes!

"Hello Chips! (As carpenters are called) How's you doing these days? It **was** a long time ago, but if I'm not mistaken …you deserted in Valparaiso."

Replying in feigned surprise:-

"Why heavens above – 'tis Cap'n Ned; 'an what ye say is right.
Ah left ma berth and got blind drunk – 'cause I thought ye'd never make Perth."

****

They sailed away a dismal sight, and as top-men freed the sails, loads of dust fell down – and stained the white scrubbed rails.

The bosun and crew soon set to and washed her from bow to stern: and Septimus Smith got soaked through an open porthole – a lesson he would learn.
On the way they passed the "*MAGNIFICENT PINE*" Another ship of the Magnificent Line. Sailing in to Cardiff Bay – to earn her living the tramp ship way!

Through the Pillars of Hercules the "*ART*" sailed on with clippers ease; then left a bit to Gibraltar; to disembark some passengers and take on fresh veg. and drinking water.
On to Gibraltar Bay – full of ships all 'navy-grey' and the Admiralty had something to say…

"A message Sir."

"What do the signals read?"

'You fly the proud red ensign, so you should feel ashamed. Remove your 'F' from your 'A' before you further proceed'

Captain Felix flew into a rage.

"Find the man …I'll have him flayed!"

Ned soon figured it out.

"The man who painted out 'F' in black, included a
dollop of the cook's pork fat. Needless to say the first
heavy sea …washed it all away!
But the man isn't enjoying much elation, having
suffered three weeks with constipation …and what is
more – has requested to see the doctor ashore."

Captain Felix replied:- "Request denied!"

Hard over once past Europa Point, and the
Mediterranean spread out ahead.
But the course chosen by the captain came as a
surprise to Ned.

"Why a course so northerly, when sailing east
through the Mediterranean Sea?
With the risk of the 'Mistral' up ahead – North African
coast safest …I would have said."

"I have my reasons, trust me Ned …better late than
everyone dead!!"

****

The days passed away most lazily as the 'ART' crept
through a glassy sea.
But Ned had open a 'weather eye' as high cirrus built

up on the Northerly sky.

And as he studied the cloud climbing high – all hell broke loose over …a rabbit **pie**!?

Mrs Smith asked:- "Can I have some pie?"
But her husband said:- "Vegetable stew is the best for you."

The captain replied:-

"Let **her** decide – the rabbit was freshly supplied in Gibraltar."

Mr Smith tried to suppress his anger.

"Mind your own business Sir that is not the way I have taught her."

****

Ned was right and the barometer fell.

"We are in for a blow – I can tell."

And by change of watch at eight o clock – the 'ART' rolled to a heavy swell.

Next came the rain and stinging hail- and the wind built up to a screaming gale. And soon 'hove-to' – only a jib and storm sail having to do.

Mr Smith screamed out in pain, he'd left the porthole

open again; his bedding now soaking wet, blamed
his misses …and gave a lecture she'd never forget.

The captain reluctantly agrees, a s'utherly heading is
what they would need; if the voyage was to progress,
North African coast was the better guess.

And so it proved and in a few days – purple and grey
in the sunset's haze.
Mr Smith said:-

"Let us make a toast, for what was once known as
The Barbary coast."

But Captain Felix was not at ease – and confided in
Ned his concern for these seas.

So it came as no surprise when above the horizon
began to rise …A triangular sail!
They watched it closely and hour by hour without
recourse it held on to – a converging course.

"As I feared Ned, something we **should** no longer
dread.
But I would bet from behind that islet, is emerging a
legendary Barbary Pirate.
Get the women down below and warn the crew what
they must do."

Ned could hardly believe his eyes.

"It's the **third** time this has happened to me – the last
was in the Arafura sea.

Where when you want them are the British **Navy**?"

****

Six guns let forth a lethal hail – a thousand holes in the mainmast sails.

"There's really nothing that we can do; bring her around Mr Ned, we must heave-to."

Ned hurried about: Jewels; watches; money to collect. Septimus Smith the one to object.

"It's **disgusting**! I cannot agree with **you**!"

"Believe me (Ned replied) The Arabs will never search inside – a pile of piggy poo!"

****

The felucca dropped its lanteen sail and Mustapha leapt over the port side rail.
Dressed as a sergeant of the Foreign Legion – followed by Sayeed – a shifty fellow …big hooked nose and teeth bright yellow.

"Hello captain: Welcome again to my region – you've arrived just right for the start of the 'shooting season' (He laughed) Not pheasants …ships of course, full of lovely presents?"

"Mustapha - we meet again. **You** are becoming a bloody pain.

Pirating is finished, your father agreed …You will
hang for your continuing greed."

"Captain: You have a nerve to accuse me of greed
and for what my father agreed. So much for British
treaties …your Navy returned and blew his town to
pieces."

Chippy knocked out the hatchway wedges, swearing
in Gaelic all the while; made old Sayeed smile who
thought it sounded Arabic!"

But then they all stepped back in shock, as they
gazed down on piles of black Welsh rock.
Mustapha was looking all confused.

"Not the stuff that I can use.
Last time you had cases of wine, tobacco and
cheeses; silk and coats made of fleeces …And with
that I made an excellent profit.
But with **this**? …It will only burn!"

The pirates searched from stem to stern – but little
looting did they earn …a different story if they only
knew, a treasure cache under a pile of poo!

Mustapha angrily paced up and down; then the
heavens opened and the rain poured down.

"I am going ashore to make quite sure that for coal
there is a market. And I give you a warning I'll take
the women and children too – so there is nothing you
can do …until I return in the morning."

Captain Felix and Ned had a brandy or two – tried to
plan just what to do.
And in the end they had to pin their hopes on the
captain's number two, telescope.

****

Early next morning the felucca arrived and the
women were helped back over the side – except Mrs
Smith!?

Septimus stepped forward in his pompous way –
nose in the air; he had things to say.

"What of my **wife**?
I guess a victim of Arab lust – you gave your word:
So much for trust!"

Mustapha replied:-

"Sorry mate, she's with Sayeed …she chose to stay
with us!"

"Now then captain, this is what you will do:
Follow me south to an anchorage that will be new to
you.
Then your men will discharge the coal – after which
you will see …I will set you free!
And just in case you try a trick, I will leave three
armed men to guard you."

And as he turned to go:

"You can keep the pigs, I'll take the chickens …and I'll have this telescope too."

****

They followed at a steady pace, a felucca too fast for them to race; and for what Ned and Felix knew – a safer distance would better do.
Mustapha – delighted with his optical prize, was having trouble to focus. He pulled again at the viewing end where the brass was strangely eroded …and that was the last thing he'd **ever** do: as the bomb inside exploded!
The armed guards eyes wide and full of fear, watched their felucca disappear.
And before they mouthed their vengeful pledges – the crew attacked with Chippy's wedges.
But as ten missiles bounced off his head – one of them shot poor Captain Felix – dead!

…The sailmaker finished the burial shroud.
And with tradition, as it goes, the last stitch through the old man's nose: He looked at Ned.

"You'll be pleased to know he felt no pain"
Then added:-
"I guess that makes you Captain again."

****

Duty done and all secure, they headed east into a boiling sun.
The handrails soon too hot to touch; no-one liking it

very much. Little wind to make them go: But trouble brewing down below.

Ned walked up and down the quarter deck. The evening breeze, the wind-chutes set, to cool the places down below: But in the lower hold ...a fire aglow.

Chippy was the first to tell:-

"Cap'n, in the fo'c'sle there's an **awful** smell; it's no Jimmy's socks 'ah can tell; but frum tha' place he hangs his coat ...Ar's seen the wisps of coal fire smoke."

Ned no more he needs to know:-

"Ring the bell, let everyone know. **Plug any way** of letting air below.
Haul in sails, let her drift; get hoses rigged.
For it is my assumption – we are experiencing spontaneous combustion."

But Chippy, not parting money with the others, had stashed a wad under the hatchboard covers. Now with a feeling of desperation, unable to bear the separation ...opened a corner of the covers – which up to then the fire it smothered.

Suddenly, the cloth too hot to handle a flame shot up like a 'Roman Candle'!

****

The 'ARK' had been a well equipped ship, so plenty
of room in the boats to fit …and they drifted aimlessly
on a glass-smooth sea; Septimus Smith in number
(3).
Who complained endlessly:-
"My belongings got soaked in the rain so to the
company I will complain.
The food consisted of too much meat and I couldn't
sleep because of the heat.
And finally to my displeasure, I'm sharing a gig with a
smelly pig …called 'Treasure'!"

Next morning: First light, nothing in sight to fix their
weary eyes on. Then young Jimmy gave a shout, his
hand pointing out …a ship coming over the horizon.

With drinking water running low and endless miles
to go; would you believe, her sister ship "*THE
MAGNIFICENT PINE*" was about to perform their
rescue.

****

Sidney Biscuit, the Ambassador's assistant whose
job was to help Brits. In distress. Found his job most
boring; thought seamen's troubles were whoring and
preferred they were under arrest.
Ned presented his papers; and Sidney examined
his chart on the wall – on a box for he wasn't too
tall …for ships that had gone missing – found "*THE
MAGNIFICENT ART*".

"I'm sorry captain that you lost your ship. The cargo I

hear overheated" …Then into Ned's book – a big red stamp: 'Voyage Not Completed'!

****

The Trampship Skipper

A dejected Ned: In Port Said, laying on his bed; a
book half read.

Three weeks since he had arrived and many ways
he had contrived to secure a berth on a 'homeward
packet' – as passenger or crew, anything would do to
get away from the dust, the smells and the racket.
Fed-up with bumboat men, spitting camels and
donkeys that kick and the gully-gully man with his
kids party tricks (never did figure out where he hid all
those chicks)?
Reduced to entertainment of cockroach races, along
the ledge at the side of his bed. They ran fastest for
a piece of cheese; other food (like Ned) they tended
to leave. The worrying part of these games …he's
starting to give the vermin names!

His room up on the third floor, surprised therefore to
hear a knock on the door.
It was Sidney Biscuit, the Ambassador's assistant
– who looked suspiciously around …expecting a
whore?

"Good evening Captain Ned, I hope you are well?"

"How **can** I be – in this back door to hell? Where is
the berth that you promised me? …I'm fed up with
waiting: and I'm missing the sea."

"The problem solved Captain … I need a good man for a steamer: Pack your bags let's be going, as soon as you can."

Ned gave a sardonic grin.

"So has this been the reason for the delay? … Sorry Sidney you've got the wrong man; I'm a **sailing ship** master – no experience of a floating tin can."

Sidney stretched to his full five foot two.

"A mere technicality when things you must do. I am a man of considerable enforcement …Here Captain Ned – your Steamship Endorsement."

****

In a moth-eaten gharry he sped down to Port Suez. Reluctantly admitting DeLessop's canal was something quite grand (Better now in Great Britain's hands). On the road, passing ships as if sailing through sand.

Ali the agent in his nightdress and fez; greeted Ned on his arrival in Suez.

"A boat is a-waiting (He spoke very good English) we mustn't delay; the steamer's been waiting for too many days.
Bound for the canal with a full cargo of coal. The owners redirected 'South America she's to go'.
For the British are building the Argentine Railway and

constantly stress: The coal for our engines must be
the best.
The ship they expected has not appeared (sunk it
is feared) and with his change of orders Captain
Fernandez disappears. Took his belongings and
three months money (He left in a bit of a hurry).
He'll have to keep running, he cannot relax; in
Rosario waiting: three angry wives, ten hungry
children and the collector of tax."

Ships of many nations, at anchor awaiting their turn –
for transit or cargo, destinations to learn.
Steamers and clippers – in ballast or loaded …one in
particular filled Ned with foreboding – "*NORBITON*" –

"That's her (Said Ali) a fine ship you will agree; the
shape of the future: will change things at sea."

"She's ugly (Ned replied) and I cannot agree; her
slab-sided construction does nothing for me …And
what on earth is covering her decks?"

"Ah …dredging equipment I strongly suspect. Bound
for Mombasa – a freight we were lucky to get.
You will just about reach there, your bunkers quite
low; but the monsoon is behind you, so you shouldn't
be slow."

****

The master's cabin – well furnished and compact,
but tongue and groove boarding made it feel more
like a shack. Mahogany furniture, louvered portholes

and doors; an Indian carpet on well scrubbed floors.
Covers and curtains all very neat …but useless and
worthless in the insufferable heat.

Ali sweating, keen to go.

"Let's check the safe, that's all I must know.
£100 sterling and 150 dollars U.S. …for
disbursements only – I must stress.
Sign here Captain …now she's over to you."

Mr Evans the First Mate knocked on the door.

"Welcome aboard Sir. Everyone's present and she's
all secure."

"Tell me Mr Evans, how do the men sleep in this
terrible heat?"

"Exhaustion more than sleep Sir –
There's **not** a cool patch: you can fry an egg easily
on number three hatch."

Ned shook his head slowly.

"All ships that I've been on would have **awnings**
secured, for heat is a problem that poor seamen
endures; the shade and the breeze, discomforts will
ease …**So why have we none**?"

Mr Evans shrugged.

"Requests were repeated …but always deleted."

"**Right** then Mr Ali – I regret further delay. I want bolts
of canvas …Egyptian cotton the best, so some folk
say."

****

Ned walked the bridge from side to side and had to
admit, a good view did provide.

"Haul away Mr Evans."

He called to the bow; to bring in the anchor …he
didn't know how, without capstan and shanties and
full sweating crew, but the sound of 'clanking' gave
him a clue.
With hissing and puffing and great clouds of steam,
over gypsy wheels of the windlass – the cable came
in.

The bell rang out loudly as the hook left the sea floor
and the third mate blew the steam whistle which let
out a roar …and if truth be said frightened the pants
off **sailing ship** Ned!
He pushed the telegraph lever to 'Slow ahead' and
the vibration told him she's no longer 'dead'. Broken
water appeared at the stern, the propeller revolving,
the bow started to turn.

"Steady she goes."

He called to the men on the big steering wheel. And
to the third mate day-dreaming.

"Haul the flags down: **if you will!**"

They set a course down the Red Sea – Mombasa bound – the main engine thumping – a new day and night sound.

The captain decided it was time to explore and came to a white-painted engineroom door …and looked inside.
Into the cavernous space in the centre of which a coffin shaped object took pride of place. Shimmering and shaking in the **infernal** heat – the main engine pistons: the ship's own heart beat.

A voice penetrated the cacophonous noise.

"Hoo sez you can enter mah engineroom door?"

Ned extended a hand.

"Hello Chief, I'm Captain Ned; I just want to explore."

"Hi Cap. – 'arm Andy O'Toole, 'an ah make it ah rule … - Nobody goes doon below …unless ah say so."

First time for Ned to be restrained on his ship – but for the time being he'll just bite his lip.

"OK then Jock – I will not stop!"

"Mr Evans – the awnings; are they ready to go?"

"I'm afraid Sir on a steamship – no sailmaker and few

who can sew."

****

Four apprentice boys on number two hatch, sat in a
row; the captain instructing:-

"I'll teach you to sew canvas, with palm and needle,
beeswax and thread; and we will rig the first awning
before time for bed"

"I want small neat stitches – in long straight seams,
double in the selvedge where the boltrope ties to the
beams, called 'awning spars' as you should know.
Now I'm making the eyelet where the lashings will
go."

Like an awning factory, they started to grow and
everyone able was wanting a go. Including the 'black
gang' who stoked boilers in their own kind of hell;
white eyes peering through sooty black faces – hard
to determine their age or their races. Liverpool-Irish
so Ned was informed, could be moody, but they kept
very calm; a little bit slow, their hands so hard they
didn't need the pad on the sailmaker palm.

The Red Sea at its shimmering worst – too hot for
movement always dying of thirst.
But passing Perrim Island at its s'utherly end:
blessed relief – the last awning was rigged with spare
canvas for hammocks, beneath which to sleep.

****

Abigail Smith (Passenger) as far as Ned could tell;
like the coal, a South Wales gal; with protruding teeth
of enormous size, staring eyes and stick-like thighs.
Sat on the boat deck enjoying the breeze.
The passage she gave her reason: "Off to help the
unwashed heathen!"
She sits around all day and is most inactive, yet to
First Mate Evans …strangely attractive.

The Gulf of Aden and discomforts eased as they
enjoyed the start of a fresh ocean breeze…
But rounding Socotra a new kind of motion as
"*NORBITON*" entered the Indian Ocean. A strong
wind a-blowing and a quarterly swell; her captain
discovers: she rolls like hell!

The second mate reported:-

"She's doing good speed – up to now six knots, she'd
rarely exceed – but by my calculations she's pushing
on eight, helped along of course by this favourable
sea state."

"But she can do better (Ned replied with a smile) I've
been looking at those yards for more than a while –
naked and waiting for a favourable wind. Bend sails
on Mr Simes …let's push her to nine!"

With black smoke belching from her tall, thin smoke
stack; white canvas stretching, stays showing no
slack.

The sails reduced her ponderous roll – something

a sailingship master knew well. Ned felt more
comfortable with this compromise, despite
"*NORBITON'S*" engine and her big freight earning
'Can go **anywhere**' size. But … running free on a
clipper – it just wouldn't compare.

****

Mombasa they made in eight days; no engine
breakdowns or other delays. In Kilindini harbour they
dropped their 'pick' – and the natives discharged the
deck cargo surprisingly quick.
Alongside came the barges with coal – she needed
plenty, her bunkers now empty.
Day and night, a pitiful sight; native boys shovelling
the coal, into wicker baskets; hot and dirty, their
conditions grim; the only relief an occasional swim.
A gang of six appealed to Ned. A cheeky youngster
by which they were led – called out "Jambo" each
time they met. White teeth flashing, jokes a-cracking.
Ned called out: "I could do with a crew like you" and
passed down a bread loaf or two, which they blended
in with their watery stew.

The bunkers full and more piled on deck for ahead
lay a very long trek …and the Chief not a happy
chap:-

"Ah dinna like this coal, it's very dirty …a load of crap
an 'ard like ta get ma hands on yon agenting chap."

Cape Town bound; time to go and the third mate
missing. Last seen in a bar, a black girl kissing.

Ned blew three long blasts on the whistle …that did
the trick! Furiously paddling dugout canoe, it cost him
his shirt, his trousers and long-johns too.

****

Ned and Mr Evans 'shot the stars' that night - what
sailors call 'taking a sight'. The position they fixed did
not bode well – barely five knots was all she could
make …a struggle indeed to meet The Cape.

But reach it they did, sweeping dust off the stokehold
plates. The agent alarmed because they were late:
confided in Ned what he already suspected.

"A long way to go with just a cargo of coal …the
railway's important, but that's not all.
This ship is also a thing of great interest – advanced
engineering is built into her, including a thing called
a 'surface condenser' …which means your steam
returns to water …fuel consumption you could not
beat …a successful voyage captain: They'll build a
whole fleet!"

"OK mister, I hear what you say: but Montevideo is a
very long way away; four thousand miles: that's a lot
of fuel and although the bunkers are big for a ship of
this size …my crew safety I will **not** compromise.
So to your associates: No back-handers – no
rubbish. Look into your soul, and fill up my bunkers
with the best steaming coal."

Abigail Smith had been shopping ashore – not Table

Mountain for her to explore. But bundles of blankets
– bags of biscuits and strange edible matter.
For cold or for hunger?
Ned convinced …she's a bit of a nutter!
Ned and O'Toole had sums to debate; with Scotch
and cigars they stayed up quite late.

"With good coal and clean boilers we must do better
than eight."

"'Tis twenty-two tons daily – 'ard sey ah most
ambitious coal rate."

"It all depends on what wind I can find; with full sails
set we'll get a push from behind.
But not in **these** latitudes, steering due west; better
go north a-while …a much better bet."

"But Cap'n tha' distance ye'll surely increase? Ah
hope yoo's know what yoo's aboot – get it wrong …
tha' fuel will run oot!"

****

 They departed Cape Town without further delay and
by sunset were clear of old Table Bay.
Then "*NORBITON*" tasted the s'utherly swell, all
the way from Antarctica …it didn't bode well. She
rolled like a mad thing, the sea crashing aboard and
pinching some coal surplus from where it was stored,
by number three hatch …it's gone overboard.

"Bottom heavy." The third mate informed.

"Bottom heavy? (Ned replied) My arse …this old tin can would roll, in a field of wet grass."

She rolled hard and to into her scuppers and in the saloon you can easily find yourself eating – the next person's supper.
Four days later and conditions are better and Ned was right, the more northerly to set her.
The wind it is fickle and hard to get, despite Ned's skill and experience and the yards hauled hard back …Then on the third day, the wind came away – helping achieve the knots he would need.

The chief's not happy and everyone's told:-

"Any rubbish combustibles doon 'ta tha' stookhold."

And to the cook:-

"Doon't throw awey any bones or any waste offal; dry it oot 'ta fit, mah stokers big shovels."

To the apprentices a challenge they couldn't ignore a chance for some mischief and pyrotechnics explore! In the dead of the night, no-one in sight; on a ladder that ran up the front of the stack, Charlie the junior carried a worn-out knapsack. The bomb they concocted full of pork fat and sheep's guts should look most impressive when it erupts. But of ship construction they had things to learn, stuck above the smoke-box it didn't immediately burn. The gasses expanded and shot up in a cloud …Charlie hanging on to the **rail** looked up with horror as it ignited the big mainmast sail.

"FIRE!" Yelled Mr Simes and cut the topping lift ropes.
"Buckets and pumps – make sure everything gets soaked."

Ned shot on deck buttoning his coat, amazed to see six black boys slither out of number two boat?

The fire was soon checked and Ned must acknowledge a plus for steamship's, steel decks.

"To **stow-away**, Jambo; is a very big crime and usually means prison or a hefty old fine. With food and water just enough for my crew …I really am most disappointed in you."

"But captain: In Mombasa you say you could use us for your crew!?"

Abigail Smith made a stuttering noise.

"Oh please captain, don't blame these poor boys. I knew before Cape Town and should have told you; but I promised to help them find a life that was new. I have been teaching them English and I provided their food; your drinking **water** is all that they use."

As if manna from heaven flying fish daily arrived and plenty of rainwater fell from the skies.

Jambo and compatriots found plenty to do, smugly

behaving as part of the crew.

And the apprentice boys, for their roman candle …
six strokes each from the bosun's broom handle!

****

Breakfast finished and a stroll around the decks; the
wind blowing strongly, all things being equal …as
good as it gets.

The seas creaming past lifted "NORBITON" high –
when a white sail on the horizon Ned did a-spy.
He rushed to the bridge – better to see …and tripped
over the third mate, reclining at ease.

"If you spent more time observing how the ship goes
– instead of your finger always exploring, what lives
up the end of your nose. You might notice a ship
overhauling …right astern. **Pay attention** young man
if you are going to learn."

Ned steadied his glass and let out a sigh …a tower of
white sails outlined with blue sky. Coming up in their
wake made poor Ned's heart ache and for a moment
in time, his thoughts went back to his grandfather's
pond and the magnificent ship of the White Swan
Line!

The officers gathered up on the bridge.

"Gentlemen, these days – a rare privilege. The
"*FLYING PIGEON*" I knew her quite well. She'll have

tea and silk pieces, fine porcelain and china as well."

She came up abeam, her signals ran up.
'London bound – and hoping the tea prices hold up.'
Stud sails and sky sails, everything set; powerfully
straining …the market to get.
And Ned felt quite envious, knowing **just** how it feels;
as she very soon showed them a clean air of heels.

But nothing at sea can be taken for granted and only
two days since the "*PIGEON*" departed – in the early
hours of Sunday morning the look-out called out a
dreaded warning:-

"A glow on the horizon, two points on the bow. A ship
she's a-burning, I know it somehow!"

Ned called down for maximum speed and for once
the old chief grudgingly agreed.
And very soon they were up to windward – Ned
manoeuvring as close as he could.
A heartbreaking sight of great distress. The "*FLYING
PIGEON*" in a terrible mess.
But as it turned out; not a total wreck …the fire
somehow contained **above** the deck.

The crew rowed Ned over in the jolly boat –
everything stinking of hot, tarry smoke.
From end to end she was a mess; the yards all
charred, the steel masts bent. Cordage gone, the
boats just frames: nothing escaped, those hungry
flames …Started by an overturned lantern and a
deck cargo of Chinese lacquer and kegs of oil paint.

Despite all this, an amazing fact: the cargo below –
all intact!!

"Captain Wells I will tow you as best as I can;
Of course it will be slow but somehow I will get you
safely to Montevideo.
In the daylight I will row over our hawser and best
cable-laid rope; make fast to **your** cable, I'm sure we
will cope."

The chief he was grinning, he knew the end game:
How long the bunkers would last, he couldn't say,
taking coal from the cargo, now **the** only way. But
coming behind them, no need to hurry: a massive
share-out of "*PIGEON'S*" huge salvage money!

Jambo and company fell in on the deck; readily
agreeing the content of Ned's message:-

"Time now boy's to work your passage."

Awnings and hammocks were all taken down,
converted into ash sacks and coal sacks for the coal
to run around.
Into the bunkers it fell from great height – in shifts
they were working all day and all night.

The tug it met them at Rio de la Plata channel buoy –
transferring the tow …a moment of joy!

"*NORBITON*" now very much light of her marks, will
re-fill her own bunkers before she departs …just a bit
further she has to go, first Buenos Aires then up river

to Rosario.

****

The officials came out in an ornate 'royal barge' – all dressed like rear admirals, all very large …from good living, for charging high fees and taking a percentage of all that they see.

"Good morning Captain Ned: I see some cargo is missing, I must calculate from what I have listed."

Despite Ned's protestations and the law of the sea. For short-landing cargo …a twenty dollar fee!

"A certificate that you have no infectious disease – that'll be five dollars please."

"And for my officers to inspect your store …that'll be five dollars more."

"And for your crew for passes ashore…"

"**I know** (replied Ned) Five dollars **more**!!"

"Ah – I see you declare …six stowaways. At five dollars each, I'm being very fair."

"Sir (Interrupted Mr Simes) they've all run ashore. (And handed Ned a letter). In here there is more."

"So captain: Six illegal entries; a serious crime. Let's look at my list – Yes …a ten dollar fine."

Ned opened the letter and was in for a shock. Six
stowaways missing …that wasn't the lot; Mr Evans
and Miss Smith have run away too – getting married
and starting a life quite new: 'As missionaries
they are going to try, helping the natives in deep
Paraguay.'

Ned turned to Mr Simes.

"You are promoted to Mate" And awaited the official:-

"Another two illegals, I'm being quite thrifty; I have
the powers captain – to charge you fifty.
But for what we've got from your store – let's say …..
just ten dollars more!"

****

Though the cargo depleted, in Rosario they were
most warmly greeted …Captain Fernandez being
one of their own.
Born in the Pampas, he went off to sea, funded by
the parents of his first wife: Emily.
Ten children raced aboard, eager and ready …only to
discover: Ned wasn't their daddy!

Three angry wives demanded back pay – all shouting
at once and would not go away.
For peace and sanity Ned emptied the safe, then
departed Rosario for a much quieter place.
Porto Alegre to the south a very short run for a
cargo of pine logs (some weighing more than a ton).
"NORBITON" well equipped with big holds and steam

winches, was very soon loaded and Ned had to agree: The steamship was winning the race, for the future at sea.

****

They finally reached Old London Town and the owners were delighted with the work Ned had done. But with a good wage and salvage, he headed ashore to search for a clipper – to go 'sailing' once more.

****

The Worrying Smile

Captain Ned stepped up on the weathered quay to view his new command.
But all he could see was a rusty wreck, floating on an oil-slicked pond.

"Tell me," He said to a man called Fred, the foreman of the quay.
"Have you seen a ship with a raking mast by the name of "*ROSIE LEE*"?"

Fred spat in the dust between his boots and pointed with a chewed cigar.

"That's 'er," He said, "She's an evil ship – the **worst** I've seen by far."

And quietly he asserted.

"Get out while you can, for I warn you my man – the rats have just deserted."

****

On a splintered deck he spied a lad, all acne and skinny long arms …with a shaven head and an ugly rash. And a boil covered with a dirty plaster.

"Take my bags young man and show me my quarters, for I am your brand new master. And now

that I've taken a closer look – I think you should see
a doctor."
Out of the shadows stepped an oily rag in slippers
and a tartan cap.

"I'm yer chief." It said holding out a wizened hand
and speaking with a bronchial hack.

"I'm a Scot and I'm proud there's something ye
should know. Doon't expect too much, for she's a
wee bit old and more than a wee bit slow."

Then through a cloud of steam – from an open galley
door …Ned took a double take.
Three hundred pounds of sweaty flesh, a strange
moving chest in an Air-tex vest; golden curls upon his
head. Puckered lips …was the cook – called Brian!
Who gave a worrying smile.

****

They sailed away for eight weeks and a day – and
the rusty old tramp sorely tested Ned as it wallowed
all over the ocean. He fell out of bed and bashed his
head, for she rolled with a terrible motion.

But more worrying still, the crew turning ill with food
becoming atrocious.

Brian had done his best with the victualling chest,
passed on by the previous skipper.
But the crew had had enough, of weevils in the duff
and a curry made of custard and kipper.

Ned spoke to his cook in his Air-tex vest, puckered
lips and wobbling chest.

"Let us talk for a while."

And he did his best to ignore the worrying smile.

"I'll buy some stores, but I want to see things **better**
in this department. No more watery soup or chicken
from the coup that died of natural causes."

The smile it went and the face turned red.
The captain guessed it was something he'd said?
Then with a mournful cry Brian turned and fled –
spilling the marrowfat peas. And he thought he heard
a hysterical voice …"I only wanted to please."

Next day at the table and past one o' clock. Cutting
bread like concrete though the stores are now well
stocked. No sign of his dinner or even his beer.

"Tell me young man (who was scratching his rash)
where is my dinner – my bangers and mash?"

"You upset the cook sir; he's in a terrible plight, been
moaning and groaning and crying all night,"

"That's **IT**!" said the captain. "I've had quite enough.
I'll log him and fine him – I'll show him I'm tough."

He stormed to Brian's cabin, his whiskers a-tremble.
Fists tight clenched …big boots banged the floor.

"Open up you big sissy!" He roared at the door.
"You're causing a mutiny, I'll have it no more."

With a punch like a hammer, wood split asunder.
Ned entered and froze …eyes popping with wonder.
He'd sailed every ocean, seen every sight: delivered
a baby. Knew wrong from right.
But now he was caught, without hint or suspicion …
as he gazed at his cook …fulsome, taunting …aper-
ition.
And all the while, that worrying smile.

Three hundred pounds of **trembling** flesh – the Air-
tex vest upon the deck. Golden curls that did not flow
but clearly matched those, down below!
And all the while …that worrying smile.

Ned scratched his head – his face quite red – his
anger fell. He cleared his throat …took a deep breath
and said.

"Brian …you're a GEL'."

He hit the rum for the next three days, which had
never been his style. But troubled at night by that
haunting sight …and the lingering, worrying smile.

Then the night that was to change his life, the night
of the terrible storm; when the old ship crashed upon
a hidden reef – and smashed itself to pieces.

No chance would there be in that raging sea – too far
to swim to the shore.

Ned gave a sigh and saw his life flash by as he
prepared for the final gasp.
So with salt in his eyes it was a big surprise, when a
voice called out …"Coo …eee!"

It was Brian floating by – all pink and trim, as buoyant
as a well-built boat…
The only thing from that fearful wreck, complete
enough to float.

"Climb aboard," She called, "There's plenty of room
and I will sail us to the shore."

With her breasts held high to catch the wind she
steered with skill and style. And Ned held on in an
intimate embrace, for he knew it would take a while.
And he saw a cheeky grin …with that lingering,
worrying smile.

****

They lay on the beach as the moon drifted by with a
feeling of great relief.
And Ned held her hand and was feeling rather grand
that she had saved him from the reef.

He let out a sigh and knew the reason why, that
despite the trouble and strife.
He'd go on his knees and if she please …would take
her for his wife.

And he looked up at the stars above, for finally he
understood …that all the while, that worrying smile

was simply Brian in **Love**?

Then over the storm came the sound of escaping, screaming steam.
And through the surf, her bow a-gleam the "*ROSIE LEE*" was **following** him!

He could not move out of the way. He tried to speak to Brian, tried to say ...but could only stand and stare.

Then woke up from a **terrible** nightmare!

****

The Viking Virgin

Captain Ned decided to take some leave; a change from the sea – enjoy some shady trees and cups of tea.
But before a chance to walk the prom – a short-trip offer came along.

The agent said:-

"Please do me a favour Ned – for I have got a problem.
A Baltic trader is stuck in Hull. Her drunken captain's gone missing **would** you believe? And she must be in Stockholm …before the big winter freeze."

Ned gave it some thought, tempted by the generous fee and the chance to sail the Baltic Sea: 'The lands of the midnight sun'
So he accepted …deal done.

****

Down on the dock, turned eleven o'clock, the handsome ship awaited.
He cleared his throat and read the name …and read it again. The "*VIKING VIRGIN*" (Not "*VULCAN*" as the agent had said) – in rich gold leaf – beautifully carved and with bold relief.

Up on deck and feeling tired, but a bit of refreshment

needed before he retired. He entered a door which
led to the stern; Swedish names of the cabins, he'd
have to learn.

"Ah" He said "That must be the one for me – but
damn it all - there is no key."

No sight or sound of officers or crew – but he was
joining ...**surely** they knew?

At the entrance to an open door he met Eric; he'd
never heard a cat that snored before. He was big and
fat, spoiled and much too slow to catch a rat.

He ventured down to the crew's messroom ...a very
strong smell of good perfume?
And of the future he did despair – bloomers and
petticoats **every**where.
The women of Hull couldn't make it plainer, all in bed
with a Swedish sailor.
And in the morning he will let it be said: "Things will
be different under Captain Ned!"

He scratched his head, something didn't make
sense?
Gentle snoring, bunk curtains drawn. Everything tidy
and spotlessly clean ...the strangest fo'c'sle **he'd**
ever seen.

He cleared his throat and with his captain's voice,
gave an order ...they had no choice:

"Turn out right now, I'm your captain new, I have
a job for some-one to do. Break down my door, or

make it free; the last bloke left with a cabin key."

From under a curtain an arm reached out …Ned
looked hard in the shadows to see …from a hand
dangling- his cabin key.
Shapely and slender – soft and tender reminded Ned
of the other gender. Giggles from behind the curtain
rails.

He went on deck in a bit of a hurry, turned and said:-

"I don't think your game is very funny. You will find
I'm a man of the disciplined kind. So you'd better
leave the girls behind."

Next morning a little bit foggy.
Up on deck in the cold and the wet they turned out
one by one. All dressed up in big fur coats, leather
boots and woolly hats with fluffy **ear** flaps …and
gloves! And worrying to Ned – their voices most
effeminate.

One stepped forward, taller than the rest; blue eyes
smiling – most beguiling?

"I am the First Mate – pleased to meet you. Tell me
what you want and I will order the crew."

****

"Let go the moorings and haul to the lock. The tide is
falling, we must make eight o'clock."
At half past seven they were next in line. Ned was

pleased, plenty of time. And to the lockmaster he
presented his papers …who turned and said:-

"It's half past seven and you've lost your slot. It's too
late for the gate …you'll have to wait."

Ned exploded with expletives, the things sailors say.
The lockmaster shrugged and turned away.

He gave the news to the crew and the mate.

"Too late for der gate? …We will all be late and dat's
not good."
And with a wink, "Jus leave it to mee."

Five minutes later, out of the messroom door.

"Where on earth did **she** come from?"

Ned just couldn't believe his eyes. Long blonde hair,
stick-out breasts and powerful thighs. She headed off
to the lockmaster's office.
She was only gone for a little while, climbing back
aboard with a cheeky smile.

"Everything now ees alright, tho' time for the tide is
very slim ...He didn't put up much of a fight …I had
no trouble persuading heem."

Soon indistinguishable from the others …Ned would
always recognise that cheeky grin!

****

He thought the pilot very odd; every helm order
followed a wink and a nod.

"Alright for **you** eh? …this trip …just look around,
and take your pick"

Nod nod – wink wink!

Ned let out a weary sigh.

"Shouldn't have agreed, but I did, so really must try."

But nearly exploded when he saw the bosun kiss the
pilot 'Good-bye."
Out in the grey and cold North Sea, the wind blew
strong northeasterly.
And Ned was in for another shock, the skill with
which the crew undertook. Strength and competence
they did not lack as the "*VIRGIN*" went from tack to
tack.

But an awful suspicion was creeping in …a bit of
information the agent kept from him. For if correct
the agent knew, he'd never join a ship with a **female**
crew!

He turned to the tall, blue-eyed first mate.

"Some sailing orders I would like to relate – get
written down before it's too late …Oh, and include
your name, I'm bound to forget."

The mate extended a hand.

"I'm Brigette!!"

And she gave her captain a long hard stare.

"Of women sailors we don't think you care – just like English captains **everywhere**. Of your opinion do not hasten ...being women, we will not listen."

The crew they made a slow approach, removing hats, undoing coats.
Ned looked up at the mainmast shroud.
'Time to make old Nelson proud."

"You may voice **your** opinions, you may try to be bold, but whilst I am your captain ...you will do as you are **told**!"

He took another deep breath.
"The sea's no place for a lady; it's cooking and feeding the baby. Your muscles weak, your hands are soft, and you're just not build for going aloft."

One stepped forward.

"I am your bosun Eva. I'm not Swedish, I am German. If dat is vot you tink of vomen – I think we 'ave to give **you** some learning.
Tho' you vare da captain's rig – you are as they say on **your** country, a honky, chauvenis' pig!"

Up on his heels the captain rose – his face bright red, thought he'd explode.

Brigette stepped between the bosun and Ned.

"Sorry captain for what she said. But there's more
to us than bottoms and tits – we actually have some
other bits."

She turned to the crew, she'd had her say.

"Go **to** it girls, let's show we are as good as the boys
any old day.
Up aloft, let the topsail free. Haul on the braces,
show her the sea…
Set another jib don't let me down.
Haul harder Hilda 'till your bloomers fall down."

Poor Captain Ned, full of regret; never seen sails
more smartly set.

****

Ready for breakfast of bacon and egg. Ned reckoned
it was because of something he said.
For all that was offered, for him to tackle, some
excellent bread and a plate of pickled mackerel.

****

Time went by and he had to admit, he had little to do
on this well run ship.
And of the crew he was amused, some of their
methods tho' hard to enthuse.
Like sliding down the stays from up above – the yard
girls wearing, Fair Isle gloves!?

Yet sweating down the topping lift – never a care for
their 'dainty bits'.
And as Brigette put it – with a wink:-

"They're good at rope-work, knots and splices and
other – not so nautical …Nordic vices!"

And other things as he would learn – giving our
captain unexpected concern; as on the day:-
Strolling the deck contentedly, watched the wake
around them flow. Pushing along at a steady ten
knots, the "*VIKING VIRGIN*" could certainly go.

Then suddenly, a sight that wrenched his belly – a
sight all seaman dread, SMOKE coming from a fire
down below …curling from an open skylight.

He rushed to the crew's messroom, a fire-bucket in
each hand – and just for the hell of it, another, full of
sand.
From around the door, curling up and about …the
seat of the fire? He let out a shout.

"I'm coming in!"

He hurled the water without a care, over three naked
women who were sitting there …he gave them quite
a fright.
Ned's eyes opened wide …What a sight …followed
by hysterical laughter and squeals of delight.

"Captain – join us in our sauna."

"My **God**!" He said, "What a shock for a man to receive."

But just before he turned and fled …on the table a document his eagle eye perceived:
And he was in for **another** shock: and hardly believed what he just read:- 'SWEEPSTAKE'
They're taking bets on Captain Ned. 'Who will be the first to get him in bed!!?'

"Is this what they call Nordic fun? …and oh **my God** Eva's got odds of ten to one!"

He raced on deck – his face bright red.

****

But now he must concentrate most seriously – preparing for entry to the Baltic sea.

****

They raced into the Skagerrak, but very soon the westerly backed. He needed the wind to blow a bit more, to help him round the deadly Skaw.

This can be a dangerous place, and many problems to embrace; fast running current and strong rip tides. Seaweed covered rocks that old Neptune hides and the Sirens sing a mournful tune …for the mariner who fails to leave enough room.

The crew performed magnificently – changing sails

and hauling lines, a joy to see, so that he could
catch the smallest breeze, as down the Kattegat they
sailed with ease.
Finally and the very worst bit – the Oresund narrows
to Sweden's s'utherly tip. Then Trelleborg and the
open sea.

Ned gave a sigh – things looked alright as best he
could tell. Then Brigette pressed close:-

"Captain – you did very well. Your very first trip to the
Baltic sea, you handled the ship most expertly …and
tonight, we will **celebrate**!"

The dining table set out that night – beautifully
decorated and romantic in the soft candlelight.
But at each place setting all Ned could see was
smorgasbord and food from the sea.
Then his eyes drifted on a bit …at the captain's place
– a very full plate of steak and chips.
He sat down slowly.

"You are all far too good to me."

And the girls cheered and clapped most noisily.

****

There followed a crisis, no ifs or maybe: Lena the
cook was having a baby!
Nothing in the medical guide or previous experience
from which to hide. Ned rolled up his sleeves and did
his bit until seeing the little 'un fed.

And Lena called the baby – Ned.

He was just settling down – when cries of pain?

"No problem captain …Hilda's just broke a nail
again."

****

Next morning and problems of a different kind: into
thin ice the "VIRGIN" began to grind.
But she was built most sturdily and the maritime
world could give no tips to descendants of the
builders of Viking ships.

Hour by hour the ice got thicker – made Ned's fingers
fidget …then the fog set in …But comforting words
from First Mate Brigette.

"Don't worry captain; I've written in the log 'We are
entering fog – and soundings we are taking'"

Then just at the moment it began to snow. A hell of a
commotion from down below.
Ned's heart it skipped a beat and he leapt up out of
his pilot's seat.
All were shouting at the same time-: Tempers
bristling, no-one listening – some feet stamping;
Ursula ranting. Eva waving a big white '**comb**'?

"Ladies, ladies what's this all about?
No need to scream or punch and shout.
I'll be the judge, I'll stand alone. So what **is** the story

behind this comb? Ursula?"
"Eva stole it, the bliddy whore – not der firs' time, is
'appened before. It was given me by a Viking Trust
…carved out of, a walrus tusk."

Eva retorted with a Germanic rasp.

"Vikin' Trust? – my arse. More reward for Vikin' lust!"

"Now then Eva. You've impressed me as a seaman;
as good as any man. So why now do you behave like
a scratchy old hen?"

He tried to smile, the tension relieve.

"This incident I have never conceived."

"**Conceive**! She could'na conceive – she dunna
know how …the bliddy 'ol cow!"

****

Back on deck and little improvement. No soundings
yet and not much movement.
More comforting words from the first mate.

"Don't worry captain, I know this sea – the changes
they come most regularly.
There is no cloud, we'll soon see the sun and then
we make a decent run.
With a lifting breeze, we will increase our speed …
and look over there – Bornholm!"

A beautiful island rose out of the mist; calmed everyone down. Eva gave Ursula a kiss.

"And another bit of advice I'd like you to know; about the mayhem down below. It's nothing to do with women at sea, it's simply a case of PMT!"

"Approaching Stockholm rocks some call the Speckled Hen. Be very careful passing them. Not too fast, not too slow – **that's** the way to go …Just like we girls prefer our men!"

****

Tied up and safe – Schnapps by the case; a party was soon in full swing.

Out of their coats and thick woolly hats; blond hair combed waist length, some in tight plats.
Some dancing, some singing – some ringing sleigh bells.

Ned drank his share and tried not to stare: no longer his crew but beautiful girls. With their Swedish good looks …you could easily get hooked.

And then he remembered: His name in **the book**!

"**That** is not fun!"

Then Eva whispered:-

"Brigette is now favourite – odds two to one!!"

So with a nervous sigh – Time for a speech.
With a spoon tapping his cup, the girls all looked up,
with cheeky looks in their eyes.

"An experience ladies, you have given me. I will
never forget you as I travel the seas.
You handle a ship, the best I've seen. And I have
never seen a vessel more tidy and clean.
But: Sailing with women, is not for me."

"Never-the-less I salute and toast "*The VIKING
VIRGIN*""

****

And as one the crew replied:-

"The only one in Stockholm!"

****

Next day, he sailed for home on a steamer.

****

A Problem With Mail

Times are a-changing for sailing ship masters –
including our own Captain Ned.

For dependence on wind – so it is said, is making
owners turn to steam-power instead.
One new decision – once full of derision when a
clipper sailed at more than ten knots. Is the carriage
of **Mails** independent of sails …for stormy or fine, a
steamer more likely to arrive there on time.

Regular mails and all that entails is changing
business all over the world. Ship owners too – who
rely on the screw can book cargoes confidently,
ahead.

A regular letter, once a thing of pure chance, is
becoming a thing to consider; but there's a down-
side of course, for you have little recourse to
respond to problems at home. Weeks or months may
have passed to discover there was a problem – to
helplessly worry over.

As in the case of the 2nd. Mate Bill Gedd, who in
great distress looked for guidance from those more
experienced, such as his own Captain Ned.

A knock at the door:

"Come in Mister Gedd – your expression says **you**
have a problem?"

Gedd held a letter in which he had read, of
something that had happened, which filled him with
dread.

"I am sorry to trouble you – but my wife's had a baby
…that's been born …with a **Cowl** over its head?"

"Calm down now mister, for if I am to assist you –
you must keep controlled and clear …so to begin,
let's make a list of what's been said."

"Looking through my Medical Guide, 'Childbirth' a
subject they mostly hide.
It simply says:- 'A cheap whisky might sedate her'.
But there is nothing about a tin ventilator."

"The trouble you see – it's not often at sea that you
are asked to deliver a baby …Perhaps the best
advice about a mechanical device …is to ask the
chief engineer."

The old Geordie man with his dripping oil can, looked
long and hard and thoughtful.

"I doon't want ta be rood, but if she ate lots 'a tinned food, it being the main substance provider, too much tin could form a toobe within 'an around tha' bairns head inside her."

The Chief's Assistant Josh Simeon was keen to give his opinion.

"Was the vent made of tin or of copper?; for if she sucked nuts and bolts (they get cravings you know) her womb would revolt …somebody should have stopped her."

The cook had a look in his recipe book under the heading of 'Exotics'. But came to the conclusion that the shape it made …not a vent but something erotic!

The bosun made his contribution with extracts from the Seamanship Manual.
And the Brazilian Lamp Trimmer Big Ludo said, he'd heard it before … "A typical case of voodoo!"

Then another ship with mail:-

"Captain, again I must prevail. A letter this time from my wife's older sister:
Says that the cowl it is shrivelling and she's been offered ten shillings by a superstitious old sailing ship man?"

"That's **it**!" (Said the captain) I'm fed up with guessing, another opinion we need."

They couldn't agree on the best way to help her –
except that it must have been hell …to give birth to a
tin ventilator.

They trouped ashore in single file to find the house of
old doctor Reed.
They've had their say, but at the end of the day it's
professional advice they need.

****

The doctor looked over his pince-nez specs and
regarded his seafaring patients.

"Please tell me your troubles – I've no time to 'chat'.
Did you use the same woman? …Have you all got
the clap?"

He ruffled Ned's feathers.

"Steady on Doc, mind where yer at."

"So what is the collective problem?
You're standing in line – and frankly wasting my time
over a story that's complete and utter rubbish.
Your ignorance amazes – of childbirth and ladies and
it is my submission that an old superstition, a sailor
would pay more than a pound – for a shrivelled old
relic, secure in his pocket …meant that he'd never
drown.

The diagnosis I make is: a **Spelling Mistake**.
The covering of which you mention is a birth

membrane over the head of the child: NOT made of copper, tin or lead …it's a 'CAUL not a 'COWL'.

That'll be a guinea – pay on the way out."

****

The Spritsail Barge

There comes a time in a shipmaster's life when he
needs a rest from driving and strife.
A break from the sea.
Not easy, if you've no home, family or wife.

A riverside pub, just past the stall selling cockles and
whelks – he'd been told by someone, who'd been
told by somebody else.

THE SAILORS GAITERS.
Not the smartest of establishments: Garden gate
broken, weeds growing up to your waist.

"You'll be 'appy 'ere Sir."

Said the cabby, whose horse found the roses just to
his taste.

The pub sign creaked lazily in the warm afternoon
air, like the half-timbered building …in need of repair.

The landlord proudly showed Ned his number one
room, with cheap chintzy curtains and wide river
views.
With a kitchen cloth he took a swipe at the cat curled
up on the double sized bed – looking dead …leapt
three feet vertically, banging its head.
Pulling back the covers to show sheets ironed and
clean, and with a lascivious wink…

"You don't need to be lonely sur, if you know what I mean!"

The landlady brought Ned another tankard of ale as he looked out on the river …a barge fighting the tide, struggling to sail.
He stretched out his legs, laid back in the large wicker chair …the smell of tonight's dinner faintly caught in the air.
The sound of a chain running out …somewhere over there.

****

His sleep was disturbed.
A boat running up on the gravely shore; the rower grumbling and cursing, he'd beached here before.
He stopped beside Ned.

"Looking for a job mate?"

Before Ned could reply, the landlady made a hasty appearance.

"Now then Big Jim, don' you go disturbin' moi guest – an tuck in yer shirt, yer showin' yer vest."

Ned held up a hand, a little amused.

"A bargeman I'm not, you must be confused."

"Apologies sir, tis desperate I am, I've a cargo to collect and I'm short of a man."

He pointed to the spritsail barge tugging at its anchor chain.
Ned yawned.

"Men are drinking in the bar – you'll not have to look very far."

"Farmers and army deserters – that's who they'll be – but I can tell at a glance, **you're** a man of the sea."

Ned shook his head.

"Sorry my friend, I'm taking a rest …surely, to sail a **barge** you don't need the best?"

They talked for a while and Ned warmed to the bargee, realising that big ships or small ships, you're all slaves of the sea.

"Well, you can't do 'owt for five hours or more, the tide being hard on the flood. So won't you join me my friend, at my table for some wine and some landlubber's grub?"

They talked long into the night, of storms and strange places, of difficult navigation and crew.
They drank full and hearty and ordered extra portions of the landlady's fine rabbit stew.

The barge "*KATHLEEN*" swung slowly at full tide – her chain churning the mud, now the ebb she would ride.

Big Jim weaved unsteadily to locate his boat, fell flat
on his face, tripping over a rope.
Ned focused through one good eye.

"You're not fit to row man …don't even try."

****

Next morning the landlady called at eight o' clock
sharp; pulling back the curtains …dust filled the air.
Ned flat on his back, Big Jim stretched out on a chair.

She shook Big Jim roughly.

"Do'n think you can spend the night 'ere for free moi
lad."
Ned awoke – not in the best of mood.

"Away with you woman, get us drink and some food."

"Not for 'im I won't."

"Madam: I paid for this room and according to your
husband …I didn't need to be alone."

"That d'on include barge people …it's extra two
shillin' I want."

Ned thought for a moment …then with a quarterdeck
voice:-

"Madam. You have just lost a fortnight's rent for this
(he scratched) flea-ridden room. So write up my

slate.
Big Jim …you've got yourself a new first mate."

They rowed to the "*KATHLEEN*" ; expletives from the pub management loud in their wake.

****

Ned was surprised by her size and solid construction. A huge main mast with heavy canvas sails secured in a seaman-like way. One hundred tons as best he could tell …concentration difficult due to a most awful smell.

Big Jim grinned.

"No tea clipper this Ned – instead London's finest dung! Inward we was full of hay, now we take back to the Suffolk farmers; the stuff 'recycled' – shall we say."

They descended into the aft cabin – its own homely smell of cooking and new rope.
Two bunks, a stove, cupboards and seat. Polished brass, china, all shipshape and neat. Reminded Ned of a Gipsy caravan …home for a woman, a boy and a man.

Jim proudly spread his calloused big hands.

"My 'ome and my father's before me: also my wife and the mate, trouble is 'es only eight and is sick – so she's stay'in with 'er sister.

We've a favourable wind so let's heave up and away.
I'll show you the ropes ...you'll know anyway."

Ned cranked the dolly winch handle that brought in
the chain – the pawl clinked steadily ...it started to
rain.

Big Jim was everywhere letting go lashings, hauling
on ropes; securing the main sheet, foot on the wheel
spokes.
"*KATHLEEN*" was suddenly free and she fell away
to the tide. But Big Jim turned her expertly and she
leaned to one side.

"Let go the port lee-board Ned, if you will. We'll take
West Thurrock up close, then the main sail will fill.
Ease out the head'sle, haul on that sheet.
Here we come Lowestoft – good riddance Purfleet."

The tackle squeaked as Ned eased down the heavy
lee-board; tarred and iron strapped, showing some
weed – gives flat bottomed "*KATHLEEN*" the 'grip'
she will need.

"I confess (he said) there's more to sailing a barge
than I'd given credit; there's a lot to do for your wife,
your son and you."

Passing Gravesend and she's running well.

"Take the helm Ned and I'll set up a jib. Seven knots
she's doing as best I can tell.
It's sixty-five miles to Harwich. If the wind holds and

the tide's right, I think we'll manage."

The lower reach of the river faded away, the sun
settling on London, a red end to the day.
Big Jim getting some sleep. Ned familiar with the
estuary and the North Channel leading out to the sea
...a watch easy to keep.
With night the wind eased and the ebb faded away –
and in the dark Big Jim's voice.

"I think 'ere we will stay. Foulness Point to port – not
a bad place to wait; a good run tomorrow, we'll not be
late.
Let go the anchor Ned, I'll take in the sails. Secure
for the night is all we can do. Waiting below is an ale
and a pot of dumplings and stew."

They both snored through the night and were up at
first light ...Ned soon requiring the loo.
Big Jim grinned – nodded to a bucket in the corner.

"On a barge Ned, **that** 'as to do!"

"I've set up the spanker, will push 'er arse round.
Bring short the anchor, it's good holding ground ...
then a hand with the mains'ul, make a good tight fit
...out with the topsu'l – press on the sprit."

The coast of Essex peered through the mist; the
breeze fresh westerly gave "*KATHLEEN*" a lift as Big
Jim swung her north easterly ...she started to shift.

"We must make Clacton before the next half tide – or

another night at anchor we'll have to ride. But that's too risky: I've one hundred tons of bricks booked for Putney; but the shippers they don't care …another barge will pinch my fare."

"Bricks?" (Ned asked, surprised).

"Aye. We're helping to build London, good freight but hard work loaded and discharged by hand.
The wife uses canvas mittens, but they don't last for long. When a bargeman looks for a wife, it's nice that she's pretty but she has to be strong. There's easier stuff, like barrels of oil or fish. Sugar, timber and feed – even mud and clay but that's work you hope not to need."

****

The lights of Clacton four points on the bow – she's making good time, goodness knows how for she's pushing the tide and the wind's starting to back.

"Stand by Ned – get ready to tack."

A steamer from Ipswich crossed over their bow – Jim hauled to the west for local know-how.
Keeping the course nice and steady, he knew where to find a northerly eddy.
But success at sea is between skill and God …the wind fell away and they ran into fog.

Ned realised Big Jim was having a test, the last land they'd seen was Oford Ness …close!

"We've got the ebb, a chance I must take – a stern anchor I can use – acts like a brake!"

Ned's master's instincts he could not ignore – for certain he heard wavelets on a close stony shore.

"Jim, it's coming in thick – don't you think we should stop and drop the pick?"

"Go forward Ned, watch and see if the lee-board trembles …and throw these as far as you can."

He handed Ned a bucket of pebbles:

"A 'splash' is alright – then throw some more …a 'clink' means we're too close to that damned old shore."

A fishing boat crossed ahead and her letters Big Jim clearly read, suggested they were near Old Southwold. Big Jim's face relaxed.

"I'm pushing her head offshore, no need for pebbles any more Ned; a couple more hours you'll be in your bed."

A broad run in is what Big Jim needed – but old King Neptune superseded and *"KATHLEEN'S"* pace was very slow – the last of the tide …a mile to go.

Out of the fog shapes appeared – the harbour inviting as they neared: But the big sails failed in the final light airs …the depth slowly falling …they need more than prayers.

"Someone's calling – he's rather small – standing above the harbour wall."

"That's wee Tommy Tinker, as wide as he's tall. A tough little 'Huffler' – would give us a pull …up to the berth, but he charges the earth.
A final favour I'd ask of you Ned. Take the boat and small 'pick' and row ahead.
I'll pay out a light bass line …a hundred feet would do just fine. Then drop the pick and I'll haul her on."

Five times Ned rowed the line towards the berth, finally securing it to the earth. Then Big Jim cranked the dolly winch and through fine mud they slid …inch by inch.
At last secured and plain to see …thousands of bricks stacked evenly.
At six AM some help at last; uncover the hatch Ned's final task.
They parted on the cobbled quay, shaking hands emotionally.

"As a deep sea man through and through I've admired things that you must do …simply to earn a bob or two. Big ships, small ships, I've sailed them all and amongst all seamen Big Jim …**you** stand tall."

****

The Admiral Of The Ocean Seas

31 degrees north.68 and a half west according
to Ned's forenoon calculations, but a mist had
softened the southern horizon – giving the sextant a
questionable angle.

"Not surprising (muttered Ned) it's what I'd expect,
for we're in that cursed Bermuda Triangle."

Each time he's crossed that mysterious patch,
misfortune came for a ride; a cabin boy got deliriums
and another fell over the side.
One thing never changes he was reminded, 'sweat-
stuck' to the chartroom seat, was the unreliability of
his compass plus unrelenting, pitch-melting heat.

With a cargo of bagged cane sugar and best-crop
coffee beans, smelling like a warehouse – he must
make New York's market, using every fitful breeze.
Water tasting rancid, the salt-pork beginning to
'move'. Just an occasional zephyr, the sea as if it
were glue.

"Sail Ho!"

A rending sound as Ned parted his seat; he'd
reached for his trusty old spy-glass.

"Sod it (he cursed out loudly) feels like I've just torn
the skin off my arse."

****

"Where away Mr Mate?"
"Four points to starboard, at right angles to our
northerly track. The strangest craft I've ever seen,
must be from Africa or somewhere like that?"

Many hours would pass for a closing; speculation
from stem to stern. Ned had never seen such
concentration from a crew usually unwilling to learn.
They'd started taking wagers, on what it could
possibly be: favourite was a 'floating carnival',
somehow got blown out to sea.

Now just a couple of cables.

"Blast him for his cheek standing-on. Hard down,
Mister, man the braces – we're coming around."

Avoiding a close situation, Ned was angry that it had
to be done; so imagine his utter amazement when
the other let fly with his gun.
Scrap metal, stones and other rubbish, clattered
harmlessly against the ship's side.

"The devil, he's using a swivel; a relic of days gone
by. Quickly, fetch me my shotgun ...he'll wish he
hadn't tried."

Ned aimed deliberately high.

'Bang' – Straight through the mains'ul topping-lift; the
sail itself peppered with holes. Then a crash that sent
them scattering as the yard fell into the hold.

Ned adjusted the spy-glass focus – he could hardly
believe his eyes: the crew in medieval costume,
armed with pikes, swords and long curved knives.

"Heavens – they're **Pirates** – in fancy dress, and look
like they're ready to fight.
In all my days seafaring, I've never seen such a
fanciful sight."

Three shotguns levelled on the bulwark.

"Take aim, but try not to kill. Let's cut his rigging to
pieces, that'll leave him standing still …But first,
show 'em our ensign."

It soon proudly flew from the yard.

****

"Well shiver 'me barnacled timbers – they've given in
…they're playing charades."

Their ensign was struck to the main deck, a flag no-
one recognised – as big as a mizzen topgallant, a
most impressive size.

They lowered a boat and six men boarded, two in
fancy dress and they crossed the distance in no time,
the boat most skilfully oared. But Ned and his men
remained wary, for one carried an ugly great sword.

Each climbed aboard hesitantly, shifty eyes looking
everywhere – a mixture of fear and amazement: one

fixed Ned with a goggle-eyed stare.

Ned was having none of it.

"What's this game you're playing at Mister?
Firing guns from your carnival barge. Are you drunk
or just asking for trouble? …Reported, you will end
up on a charge."

The eyes grew steadily wider – the man clearly did
not understand. Then with a flourish that made Ned
jump backwards, he laid a sword across open hands.

"I think it means he's surrendering." The mate
whispered in Ned's right ear.

Then followed a babble in a language, that wasn't
any too clear.

"It's a sort of Spanish (The sailmaker volunteered) I'll
do me best to interpret …I sailed wiv 'em for a couple
of years."

"He says that he is sorry – for firing away so bold; but
thought that we are Portuguese, trying to steal his
secret new route …to Eldorado and unlimited gold."

"The man is cuckoo (Ned spoke to the mate) he
really believes this stuff. Ask him where he comes
from?"

And he stared at a sweat-stained neck ruff.

"From Palos, South West Spain. We are in the service of their majesties King Ferdinand and Queen Isabella …Under the leadership of Don Christopher Columbus."

"That does it, I've had enough! (Ned exploded) You must've been drinking salt water and…"

At that point the first mate interrupted loudly "I've got it!"
He was studying a book 'A History of Ships'.
"It's a Caravela Redonda …by now should have rotted to **bits**.
Favoured by the Portuguese and Spaniards –
reliable and fast, built to last …but that was four hundred **years** ago …still it fits.
And it goes on to say:- Chosen by Christopher Columbus looking for the New World …and Cathay?"

As if thunderstruck.

"Cathay?"

The man shrieked and burst into a fit of excitement – beyond the sailmakers ear and pointed in a westerly direction asking…

"Is **that** the course we must steer?"

"No no (Ned shook his head, grinning) keep going west you'll bump into Florida …a place for ships to steer clear."

He looked quizzical.

"Florida...? Same Hispaniola?"

"Ah (Ned spotted a clue) come look at the chart my
friend ...See Hispaniola in the Caribbean – is the Isle
of Dominica ...will **that** do?"

The man slowly mouthed the words...

"Hispaniola ...La Isla Espaniola?"

He then took on an expression – bemused!
Examining the ship and the equipment that's used.
And when Ned rolled out the chart of the Western
Atlantic ...he really began to flip.
Eyes sticking out on stalks: his finger traced the land
south to the Caribbean ...further west to the Mexican
coast. He struggled to speak ...another shriek ...

"No Cathay ...No Cathay?" His legs became wobbly
and weak.

Then – He struggled to regain his composure; stood
to attention and respectfully bowing his head, clearly
feeling embarrassed at some of the things he had
said.

"Please come and meet our leader, and if we may
copy your map, in our usual accord – you will be paid
a handsome reward."

Ned enjoying the pantomime and bursting with

curiosity – determined to prove the mate wrong
'Looking for India indeed!'
He chuckled …and agreed.

"Fine, and take this …I've no use for a sword."

****

Ned dressed in his best Sunday uniform and before
departing spoke to the mate.

"Keep those guns nice and handy Mister – goodness
knows what I'm going to see and if you observe that
I'm in trouble, let them pay for their treachery."

He and the sailmaker Sidney, stepped into the
waiting boat – not a sign of paint or putty. "How the
devil do they keep it afloat?"

Similarly the Caravela Redonda, her bleached oak
planking plain to see, even below the waterline, no
caulking to keep out the sea.
Through the crystal clear water Ned noticed, five feet
of weed grew out from her side …signs of a very long
voyage, couldn't be denied.

Once aboard he looked around cautiously, feelings
he'd never experienced before. Something intangible
and eerie – the ship's unlike any he'd seen …all
Spartan but beautifully crafted, fine lines …and the
crew watching warily, weathered skin, muscular and
lean.

The man beckoned Ned aft, holding out a manicured hand.

"Captain, my name is Vincente, I would like to call you my friend."

"Tell him (Ned turned to Sidney) we are all sons of the sea."

And held out his chart as a gesture – to copy, willingly.

Then everyone stood rigid to attention as from a shed high up on the stern castle, stepped a man of presence and importance.

Ned turned and whispered to Sidney "You don't tangle with **this** rascal."

He descended the ladder slowly; dressed in a heavily embroidered jacket which extended to his chin, with matching bloomers and stockings and a hat with a very wide brim.

A table set out at the break of the poop; a cloth of white with a cross red – and the man rolled out Ned's chart, anchoring the corners with weights …as heavy as lead.

He studied the chart as if transfixed and like Vincente before him, traced the coast southward with a hesitant hand. Stepping back with the revelation, of the impenetrable …Mexican …**Land**!!

He waved to Ned to join him and everyone visibly relaxed, and officers set about copying the chart with ink and sealing wax.

The two men shook hands firmly and Ned clearly sensed, that he was in the company of someone – of dignity and great pres**ence**.

"Or is this a floating mad house; are they all actors gone insane …because …Stand by Sidney. Here we go, they're all at it again…!"

"I am Don Christopher Columbus: Admiral of the **Ocean Seas** – Viceroy and Governor …and you Sir?"

"Oh, I'm Captain Ned, Master of "*THE CROSS-EYED RAVEN*". Bound New York with a perishable cargo; free of scurvy or other disease."

"Your ship is large and well-founded, with innovations I have never seen; and your flag is unknown to us …you must surely come from a place of **superior** race."

"Oh I don't know (Ned fidgeted a bit) She's a small 'un by today's standards; Devon is none too special; and the flag you should know is – British."

Columbus shook his head.

"British …Britannia …**English**?" (As if dumbstruck) …"Cannot be … so advanced." He pointed to the

"RAVEN".

"And your **King**?"

Ned puffed out his chest proudly.

"**Queen** ...Victoria ...Empress of the Seas."

Columbus sat into a seat heavily and invited Ned to join him, at the table set for a meal.

"Our countries do not like each other ...We fight the Moors ...you the Scots?"

"Oh, I don't know Christopher. No trouble when I was last in Barcelona and the Jocks are not a bad lot."

"Tell me (He pointed to the chart) how accurate is this and is there **no** way through to Cathay and the Great Khan?"

Ned shook his head, paying more attention to the fresh caught fish being served, smelling wonderfully of fennel and other exotic herbs ...Fine olives, fresh baked bread and a wine like syrup, thick and red. But of even more interest were the paperweights – definitely not lead!

Columbus waved and was handed a leather tube, from which he removed a parchment.

"**This** (He announced proudly) is most secret. The map of the known world, at this time. To the north belongs to Spain – to the south, Portugal …but they are treacherous swine."

Ned burst out laughing.

"Blimey mate: the world's changed a bit …I think you're out of date. There's no sign of the Pacific Ocean and the Caribbean looks like a lake!"

Columbus, no longer so accommodating and drinking heavily of the wine.

"This trip to the west my friend – is not my very first time. I found a way past Hispaniola and beyond there, the natives told …a place called Eldorado …a city made of gold."

Ned was matching him goblet for goblet.

"That's all mumbo jumbo …there's certainly gold to be found – but there is no Eldorado …you'd be better South Africa bound."

"But that is **Portuguese** (Columbus banged the table) …they keep it to themselves (His eyes narrowed) How do I know you're telling the truth?"

"Christopher, you had better believe it, there is no Indian route; and if you don't alter your course more southward, you'll not make the history books!"

With a pen he marked their position on the newly drawn parchment chart.

"Noon today Chris: you've set well to the north, take my advice and steer a southwesterly course."

Columbus tweaked the brim of his hat.

"I must confess I am perplexed – I know not what to make of this. You are clearly from somewhere advanced and strange …and no-one ever called me **Chris**!"

Ned had a slurp and filled his mouth with olives, the best he's ever known; then a sound from high in the rigging, a rustle …and the wind began to moan. Glancing to the "*RAVEN*" the mist was becoming dense, and wavelets on the surface troubled his old sea-sense. He dried his mouth on a napkin and announced:-

"Like you Chris, I'm very perplexed. I don't know if you're true or false – from now or long ago; but the weather it's a-changing so I think I'd better go."

Christopher stood and shook Ned's hand before rolling up his chart.
Then one by one he handed the weights.

"Your reward captain. Four gold ducats …Now you can retire. And if what you have told is **true** – the new face of the world will surely be down to you."

****

Back on the "*RAVEN*" and the wind had veered – the

mist was thicker, the rowers disappeared.

Ned stared at the ducats, wondering how to secure against theft, then wrapped them in a sail-cloth and double locked his sea chest.

Ten minutes later he was back on deck. The mist had cleared and of the Caravela Redonda …not a sign … not a speck.
All were scanning the northern horizon.

"Has she sunk? …Where's she gone? …in such a short while; heavens, from the top yard a man can see clearly, twenty or thirty mile."

"Back into history (The mate interjected) gone with the mist, it's what I expected."

"**Expected**! (Ned replied) what nonsense is that? I've seen it, I've touched it, believe me it is solid. If what you say is right …I've just eaten a four hundred year old olive!!"

"Let's put an end to this fantasy, it's all a pantomime; just give me a moment …I will **prove** it this time."

Back in his cabin – the chest undisturbed, both locks snapped back loudly …designed to be heard.
He unfolded the sail-cloth and was humming a song, but the tune stuck in his wind pipe…
The ducats were gone!

Clambering up on deck, the culprit to find …Who

was it knew his secret? …A certain person coming to mind.

Everyone was searching, but the situation, much worse than he had feared …Sidney the sailmaker … had simply disappeared!

****

The Final Voyage

"It's no good shaking your head Mr Ali, I know you
are telling a lie. More interested in your ten percent: I
doubt you ever tried."

Ned looked again at the agent's runner crew list.

"I'm sorry Captain Sah, tis the best that I can do.
Sailing ships are unpopular, it's hard to find a crew."

Half of Ned's men had paid-off sick, others walked
away; looking for a steamship berth, or more
convivial place to stay.

"Steamships offer an easier life Captain Sah …these
are all can be found …and only then Captain Sah,
because you're homeward bound."

"Indeed we are – if we get that far with such a motley
crew. Times are hard for sailing ships …I guess
they'll have to do."

He looked down the sorry list; including mate,
seaman and cook. Each one had been in jail, or was
in debt on a boarding house keeper's book.

****

They came aboard early next day and signed the
articles for 'keep and pay' and immediately Ned took

the mate aside – an ugly Norwegian, six foot tall and very wide.

"Listen Mister: You and I have a lot to do, making these into a reasonable crew. Your own record is not impressive... 'ignoring orders ...drinking excessive' (Ned tugged the brim of his salt stained cap) let me down once ...and as big as you are: I'll knock you flat."

The new cook failed his culinary test. With provisions fresh it should be easy – but the beef overcooked and the soup very greasy.

"We'd die of starvation before half way."

Ned quickly showed him the port gangway.

To add to his problems: A passage booked by a lady most elegant and fair – a widow, travelling alone; a Mrs A. Sinclair.
Ned knocked on her stateroom door – fidgeting, searching for words to say; but her sweet smile bowled him over, the best thing that had happened that day.

"Madam we have a problem: without a cook we cannot depart, so I regret I must transfer you, to another, more suitable craft."

"Please call me Annabel and captain do not worry. I can wait a little while longer, I'm in no particular hurry. Very few ships are leaving for London ...and I have to say, yours was the cheapest ticket, by a very long way."

Ned wasn't too sure how to take that bit of news but a cook he must pursue; in the brothels, the bars – the boarding house crimps of army deserters and inebriate crews.

About to ascend the companionway steps – her voice called from behind.

"Captain, I had a Burmese servant boy, a very fine young man. An excellent cook, hard working and honest. If you agree I will try and persuade him to join us?"

Ned's blood tingled through his salty veins – a most agreeable feeling. Not only delighted with her suggestion …but something else, most appealing.

He assembled the men under the fo'c'sle head; some sickly white, some beetroot red. He called their names one by one, for most had signed-on by the press of a thumb.

"Now listen hard: Before we leave the port of Rangoon and head out into the northeast monsoon, some facts you'd better know. I'll kick a man for sloppy work or getting aloft too slow. So if any of you think you're better than me …now's the time, to have a go."

They fitted the last hatch cover, the cargo secured

below; full to the coamings and down to her marks –
a very profitable stow.
Barrels of molasses, chutney and spice, but mostly
bags of the best quality rice.

****

They sailed away at the end of the day, down the
Irrawaddy and into the Bay of Bengal.
Ned set a course southwest to the Ten Degree
Channel …London felt a very long haul.

Free of booze and other temptations the crew settled
down fairly well. A well fed ship is a happy ship and
the cook Simon lived up to the name; he served
up meat in various ways, never twice in a week the
same.

The first hint of trouble came from the mate, he made
no effort to hide – unkempt and unshaven and breath
that smelled like a donkey's backside.

"We've a lady aboard mister; make more effort and
show respect."

The look he returned if put into words would wish
Ned was dying or dead!

Clear of the Ten Degree Channel Ned hauled her a
little more west – into the Indian Ocean her canvas
and stays to test; for the northeast monsoon was
blowing hard with a heavy following sea – and the old
"*CROSSEYED RAVEN*" lifted her skirts, making the

most of 'running free'.

Annabel sat under an awning stretched over the
teakwood poop, and she always seemed very
cheerful...volunteering to look after the chickens,
even scrubbing out their coup.

She and Ned would take afternoon tea a routine he
eagerly awaited – with endless talk of ships and the
sea and army life, his enthusiasm never sated.
It gradually dawned, it was more than just duty ...he
loved to see her in her pretty clothes: captivated by
her beauty!

The noon position fixed.
Ned watched as two men pumped the bilge; the
water fairly reeked, and he had to assure a worried
Annabel, that **every** wooden ship leaked.

He strode along the foredeck, demanding to know:
Why the pumping had stopped?

"You keep going until the suction runs dry ...and you
do it every watch."

He admonished the mate:-

"I shouldn't have to tell you, the risks if the rice gets
wet – so keep those blighters at it ...more effort:
make 'em sweat!"

He sniffed the air ...strange ...aggravating, more
than bilge water, the smell permeating?

"Let's take a look in the fo'c'sle."

What had he said that caused alarm …the first mate's frightened stare?

But everything appeared in order, in that fetid, dank, foul air …as best as he could tell.

"It surprises me mister, the crew don't complain having to live in this damned awful smell."

It was only a couple of nights later, leaning on the windward rail …a sailor appeared from the fo'c'sle, clearly very ill. He heaved up his supper and breakfast, he retched right down to his toes; a really impressive performance so far as seasickness goes. But Ned knew that wasn't the reason, it didn't require much thinking …he'd seen it all many times, the man had clearly been drinking!

"Mister Mate!"
"Bring that man to me, find out where he hides the drink." …and briefly he noticed, the man's breath and the mate's …was similarly stinking?

He stormed into the fo'c'stle, pulling men from bunks and hammocks; he turned their sea-chests inside out – but ended completely flummoxed.

Turning back he noticed, a loosened forward hatch cover? "Open it up." He ordered, thinking he had found the stash. Instead only an opened bag from the top of the fine-rice stow …but much more troubling to Ned, was the smell seeping from deep below.

To Annabel he confided.

"The smell is of contaminated rice, so I'm afraid we'll keep on stinking. But something else, be on your guard, the men are secretly drinking."

With only he and the mate to run the ship – what happened when he was below?
Ned was tempted to call into Cape Town …the Norwegian ought to go.

So far it had been easy sailing; he sighed as he eased into his bed – but soon I'll find their failings, as the wind starts coming ahead.

****

With the Cape of Good Hope now out on the beam, below the starboard horizon; the old girl rolled in the southerly swell, rail under …she started performing. And any attempt to make to the Cape would take a very long time; with the barometer steadily falling: not a helpful sign!

Ned hauled her around northwest by north – then another point west …a cautious navigational decision; for the cloud had obscured the sun and the stars – for days without a position.
The treacherous land of South Africa …and what sailors here fear the most, the cold Benguela current

with a habit, to set to the foggy Namibian coast.

Troubling news came to Ned's ear: Simon spoke of
a seaman, who complained of an alcohol hoard. Not
surprising then in the middle watch, the same man
allegedly, fell overboard?
The mate shrugged his big shoulders claims:-

"My attention was with pumping the bilge at the time
of the man's sad demise, and the suggestion of any
booze stash …just trouble-making lies."

The weather started abating, the barometer began to
rise – and a star position showed them, well into the
east, much to Ned's surprise.
At breakfast he cautioned Annabel of his decision
to search the fo'c'sle once more and if successful,
without their booze – who knows? He advised she
lock her door.

In the end it was surprisingly easy: A dripping tap!
…The water it really stank.

"**Found it**!" Ned shouted triumphantly.

"An ARAK STILL …they've used their drinking water
tank!

'DOG SWEAT' as anyone who knows will tell. Once
you become addicted …it's a one way trip to hell.
A disgusting brew, properly made with molasses and
dried red rice; but anything fermenting, even the odd
dead rat; said to cause blindness, more common a

heart attack.
Smiling, Ned took a swipe with his hammer, shearing off the locked brass tap.

Out on deck the mate was waiting, surrounded by the crew.

"Your 'devil's brew' is into the bilge …so what are you going to do? Don't think of doing me any harm, you need me to get you home …The mate will soon get the 'twitches' – you'll all be left alone."

Back in Annabel's cabin, Ned spoke of his deep concern.

"The bilge water as been allowed to get into the rice to set up the awful smell – it hid the stink of the arak; the difference you couldn't tell. **But** and this is my worry …how much? When wet, rice would begin to swell."

The answer it came shortly!

"Problems I think have started."

A shriek as a man catapulted over the side: a mainstay, it had parted.

Ned quickly seized up the situation, though it hurt his brain to accept – a disaster he had only ever heard of …a fore stay parted next.

"Get all sails off her: open hatches."

But they moved as if made of lead.

And as he spoke the hatch locking-bars broke, the tarpaulins started to shred.

"For goodness sakes she'll roll over. Cut the topping lifts, let it all go. It's all we can do to save her … there's a chance we'll get a tow."

With a 'crack' like lightning and thunder, the forward hatch spewed out bags of rice; the coamings and beams split asunder.
And from somewhere behind, a whiff of perfume – Annabel pressed into his shoulder.
Ned guided her back to the break of the poop as the main-mast – like a 'tethered bull' broke free of its stays and came crashing down, causing the fore-mast to fall.
Simon rushed out of the galley as the deckhouse tipped **up** on its side.
Crushed barrels of chutney oozed up over the deck, a malevolent, shimmering tide.
Ned then saw the bulwark split and the decks starting to bulge, as the rice grains began to double in size, no more room in those cavernous holds.

In the break of the poop they were fairly safe, only the mizzen now remained; but water was pouring through parted seams …soon they would have to leave.

Out of the corner of his eye Ned saw two men flash by with booty in their hands; they'd obviously visited his quarters: he could easily guess their plans.

An eerie peace fell over the hulk though timbers
groaned and the rice still squirmed slowly out of the
holds.
Then from under the debris of spas and sails the
remaining crew emerged; two of them wielding axes
– one of them being the mate and no longer having
to hide his shame …in a most inebriate state.
He gave orders to launch the long-boat; then turning
to Ned announced:-

"We've no further need of you; we've got your charts,
your sherry and scotch …and we'll have the woman
too."

Ned eyed the big man coldly – the treachery no
surprise. Taking out his pistol announced:-

"One step forward mister – and I will shoot you right
between the eyes."

The water now nearing the deck, the long-boat
launched over the rail; the crew stumbling over each
other, attempted to raise a sail.

****

Ned, Annabel and Simon watched them drift away.
The mizzen mast creaked and stretched its rigging …
this was a dangerous place to stay.

Luckily the jolly-boat undamaged, but needed all their

strength to clear. Ned filled it with kegs of drinking
water; food, canvass cover, compass and oars to row
and steer.
He planned to head in a westerly direction, to meet a
ship their only hope; the only other alternative: east
…onto the dreaded Skeleton Coast!

With an oar, rope and canvas, he made a make-shift
rig. Then in a heart-wrenching moment the "*CROSS-
EYED RAVEN*" finally departed, through a surface of
heaving cargo she quietly, slowly slid.

Alone on the endless ocean, for days they drifted
along. When Simon suddenly spotted a sail: was it
the one that would carry them home?

They rowed to intercept it. Annabel waved a green
silk coat: but joy soon turned to alarm when Ned
recognised, the "*RAVEN'S*" white long-boat.

His pistol loaded and ready, they rowed the last few
yards. No sign of any movement though they could
see some men's outline …and sharks slowly circled
the boat …as if …waiting to dine?

Gently they bumped alongside: they were in for
a ghastly surprise: the first mate holding the tiller
stared through dried-up, sightless eyes.
The few of the crew remaining each of them was
dead. Parchment skin and blackened for days
exposed to a merciless sun; they hadn't taken
drinking water, only whisky, sherry and rum.
Simon and Ned heaved the bodies over the side

– they mumbled a brief sailor's prayer and the
water was soon as if boiling, sharks appearing from
everywhere.

The jolly-boat secured astern; but all was not as
hoped for. The charts had been used to pack into
cracks and other surprises they'd learn.
With a biscuit and measure of water, they settled
down for the night – glad of the extra leg room and a
sense that from now …things would turn out right!?
But that hope was going to be short lived as Ned sat
up with a start; he wasn't a man to be frightened, but
now had a pounding heart.
The unmistakable sound of breakers, meant what
he had dreaded the most: That old Benguela current
had fetched them on to the Skeleton Coast. So
named for bones of ships and men …picked clean by
gulls and sun burned; very few ever returned.

He let go the jolly-boat and set up a drogue to keep
them head to sea – and the surf as much as ten feet
high pulled them in remorselessly.
Just before the sea spun them over, Ned cast out a
heaving line, attached to the drinking water cask …
he did it just in time.
He spun as if in a whirlpool, a salty, sandy hell –
and briefly he saw her green silk coat and grabbed
beloved Annabel.

"Take care of her." He shouted to Simon as he
hauled the water cask in, and luckily saved the jolly-
boat but the other was completely stoved in.
They propped the boat up with oars and rope to

give shade from the blazing sun; then all did a bit of
beach combing – Ned shooting a large sea bird with
his gun.
With plenty of wreckage to light a fire and bits of
chart retrieved, Ned used the thick glass from the
compass …a fire he soon achieved.
They ate the bird with relish; then Simon asked Ned
for his plan.

"Our situation is dire, there is nobody living here.
Our only hope is back to sea – due west we'll have to
steer.
With the desert hot and the water cold, there is
always an on-shore breeze. The chance that we
must be ready to take …is when conditions ease."

Simon shook his head.

"Of boats and the sea I've had enough – it fills my
heart with dread. I will opt to take a chance and walk
for help instead."

Ned knew that he couldn't change his mind so simply
shook his hand. And the tears flowed down Annabel's
cheeks, splashing into the pure white sand.

That night as the sun set red and gold beneath the
surf, could have been a romantic dream: but Ned
knew their chances were not too good – the worst
situation in which he'd been.
The tarpaulin folded like a mattress, they snuggled
up quite close, and turning to Annabel smiling
announced:-

"Not everything is so bad. If the old ship hadn't sunk, this is an experience I'd never have!"

"Oh I don't know (She replied coyly) I was slowly working on you; only typically you didn't notice ...but I'd have got you in the end!"

She leant over and kissed his cheek.

"I fancied you like anything ...but as a lady I had to pretend."

Thankful that it was now quite dark, she'd not see the tear trickle down his face. He wished it was somewhere else, a more appropriate place ...Now there was something he had to do.

"Annabel ...if everything had gone to plan, I'd intended to propose to you. It seems to make little difference now ...but would I have passed the test?"

She kissed him again only this time on the lips.

"My answer darling man, would definitely, been yes."

Three days had passed and as night approached the wind began to ease. The change Ned had been waiting for, and when just a gentle breeze.

"This is it Annabel, our chance to leave this place. It will still be very dangerous, we must pull through the sea and swell. But staying here is no option, we'd die in a scorching hell."

The boat lined up and ready to launch – canvas
stretched tight over the bow to stop the water
crashing in.

"This'll be no Sunday school outing."

Ready to haul as fast as they could – hesitated:
sounded like somebody shouting?

In the last of the light, from along the beach,
they saw Simon running; behind him walked two
coal-black men …completely naked …carrying
spears. Was he running from them? The situation
compounded their fears.

"Don't worry: You won't need the boat; we will be
saved by my two new friends. They found me in a
terrible state: I thought it was the end. They do not
speak any English but drew pictures in the sand –
which pointed to a township, many miles over-land."

They eventually worked their way up the coast; it
took six months for them to reach home. And to
pledge their lives to each other, they got married in
Sierra Leone.

Of twenty-three souls set out from Rangoon twenty
were dead.
And somewhere in an Atlantic current bobbed the
"*RAVEN'S*" figurehead.

****

****

The Author

Dave Wells served for more than twenty years at sea, from deckhand on a Thames river tug to master mariner.

Circumnavigating the globe several times, visiting exciting places (before package holidays and oil exploration). Sailing on WW2 tramps with just the basics provided good training in seamanship and navigation. Moving on to fast cargo liner in the latter years.

After his shipping company ceased trading he came ashore and took up garden design and construction. The sea however was always his first love.

Bibliography

Time Life books, "The Pirates" Journalists various Chapter 6.